# "Let's go to bed, Frederica."

"Poor Joe!" Freddy mocked. "You can't understand why I'm not rushing into bed with you."

"I know exactly why." Joe's voice was silky soft. "You've developed cold feet, Fred, and you've grown such a protective shell around yourself that if you don't watch out it'll smother you completely."

"And you've given yourself the task of freeing me," Freddy laughed. "You haven't changed a bit, Joe. Still so arrogantly sure of yourself."

"You have quite a good line in brush-offs, did you know, Fred?" Joe's hand dexterously removed the pins from her hair, and he began to run his fingers slowly through it. "But I know from experience that you have more fire burning beneath that cool, keep-off facade than any woman I've ever met. So why are you hiding it? What are you afraid of?"

**JACQUELINE GILBERT** began writing for the Harlequin
Presents series in 1976. She has since written
approximately one romance novel a year, a pace that
allows her a good deal of time to devote to her family. "In
the final analysis," she says, "the family is the only stable
and significant thing in our lives." She and her husband,
the person she credits most for helping her to become
the person she is today, live in England's Midlands
and count themselves lucky to have both children
and grandchildren.

## Books by Jacqueline Gilbert

### HARLEQUIN PRESENTS

### HARLEQUIN ROMANCE

Don't miss any of our special offers. Write to us at the
following address for information on our newest releases.

Harlequin Reader Service
901 Fuhrmann Blvd., P.O. Box 1397, Buffalo, NY 14240
Canadian address: P.O. Box 603,
Fort Erie, Ont. L2A 5X3

# JACQUELINE GILBERT

## sweet pretence

**Harlequin Books**

TORONTO • NEW YORK • LONDON
AMSTERDAM • PARIS • SYDNEY • HAMBURG
STOCKHOLM • ATHENS • TOKYO • MILAN

Harlequin Presents first edition May 1988
Second printing May 1988
ISBN 0-373-11073-1

Original hardcover edition published in 1987
by Mills & Boon Limited

# CHAPTER ONE

IF it had not been so important to show her face that evening Freddy would have cried off going. She had worked late on the *Tandy* rushes—which thankfully had turned out to be good so there was no problem of doing re-takes—and the rest of the day had been unusually hectic. What she really wanted to do was to soak in the bath with the last capful of apple blossom oil, read a good book, and eat scrambled eggs and crisp bacon! Pure bliss!

She frowned into the mirror and wondered if the new eye make-up was a mistake. Too late to do anything about it now; the taxi would be arriving soon and she hadn't been in to see Megan yet. She ran a brush through her shoulder-length hair and wondered if she should have it cut... Decisions, decisions, life was full of them! She pulled a rueful face and thought, hey, come on now, Frederica Leigh, stop belly-aching!

The face that gazed back at her from the mirror was not one she herself would have chosen had she had any say in the matter. Her eyes were all right, quite a nice light green, actually, but her face was too long and thin and her cheekbones stuck out too much. At least her nose was straight and her mouth reasonable, but she had the pale skin tones that gave a suggestion of frailty that was totally misleading.

The hair that she was brushing vigorously was dark brown, thick and straight with the faintest streaks of red-gold where the summer's sun had bleached it. Horse's face and mane, Freddy was wont to declare as a teenager, and the image had stuck in her mind. She didn't appreciate what prizes maturity had brought with it. Her height, which as a child had caused well concealed despair, now gave her distinction, and whatever she wore she looked good in.

She fixed ear-rings into her lobes and then a quick dab of perfume signalled she was ready. She went from her bedroom, across the hall and into her daughter's, where Megan was propped up in bed turning the pages of a picture book.

'How do I look?' Freddy asked, adopting a model-like pose.

'Nice,' declared Megan. 'All glittery like a princess. Is it a party?'

'Sort of.' Freddy sat on the edge of the bed and Megan moved to accommodate her. 'To do with work—a kind of birthday party.'

'Will there be candles on a cake?'

'I think there'll be a cake. I'll let you know about the candles. Have you cleaned your teeth—what's left of them?'

Megan bared the centre-front gap in an exaggerated smile and giggled.

'Good girl. Judith's in charge tonight. She said to tell you she'll be in to read a story in a minute.'

'Goody!' Megan's eyes lit up in her pale pixie face. Too pale? Freddy wondered with a rush of anxiety, and the usual panic swept over her, which she made an effort to contain. All children had their ups and downs, she told herself severely, and chicken pox was only four weeks back. She bent to kiss her daughter's upturned face and an onsweep of love and protection made her gather the little girl into her arms and give her a hug, whispering fiercely, 'Oooh, I do love you, Megan Leigh!'

'I love you too, Mummy,' answered Megan.

'How convenient it is that we live together,' teased Freddy, undoing the ribbons on Megan's thin, straggly plaits and pulling the hair free into corrugated waves.

'Who will be at the party—someone nice?' asked Megan, her eyes fixed on her mother's face.

'With a bit of luck, Harrison Ford,' joked Freddy, glancing at the huge poster of Indiana Jones, alias Harrison Ford, that had pride of place on the wallspace.

Megan looked at her mother uncertainly, as if unsure whether to believe that such an important film star could really be going, and then rightly judged that she was being leg-pulled and grinned. 'He's nice,' she said simply and Freddy laughed and agreed.

'He's a dish!' She gave Megan another kiss and rose, saying, 'I'll pop in again before I go,' eyeing the poster as she went out, thinking, I should be so lucky!

She made her way down the hall and into the apartment's main sitting-room, announcing, 'Judith, I think Meg is coming up for another man-hunt. I recognise the signs.'

The occupant of the room, a girl in her late twenties, looked up from the school books she was marking and sang softly, 'All I want for Christmas is my two front teeth—and a father!' Judith Snow grinned and went back to her books. She occupied the apartment above, taught sixth-form mathematics and was engaged to be married to a biochemist doing a year's research in America.

'Do you think she's insecure?' asked Freddy as she straightened Megan's school photograph on the mantelpiece and thought again what a good one it was, capturing the serious look that was especially Megan, off-set by the tentative, gappy smile.

'Kids hate to be different, and the norm is having two parents,' replied Judith matter-of-factly, marking ticks and crosses. 'If you're worried, you know what to do.'

'I'm not getting married again to provide a father for Megan,' announced Freddy emphatically. 'And she's got a father, when he remembers her. And you know I'm off marriage.'

'I'll lay odds you'll change your mind,' murmured Judith.

'I'm getting on fine by myself,' Freddy went on, ignoring her. 'I love my work. I can change a plug and mend a fuse and do other male-orientated jobs. I'm coping with Megan—thanks to you and others. I have good friends of both sexes and occasionally indulge in romantic interludes...'

'Keeping both feet firmly on the ground,' interrupted Judith, and Freddy laughed.

'Perhaps you ought to have said something different—that sounds too graphic—but yes, you're quite right. I like to call the tune these days and fit the occasional man into my life when it's convenient. Why should I get married?' She thought for a moment and went on, 'For Meggie, it's not wanting a father so much, as finding a husband for me. She thinks I'm missing out on something.' She stifled a yawn. 'I'm going to be great company tonight.'

'You'll feel different when you're there,' promised Judith. 'How I wish I had your shape,' and she eyed her friend wistfully, thinking of her own short, slightly plump form. She would have looked ridiculous in the red sequinned top and pencil-slim skirt—you needed legs that went on for ever and a height of five-eight for that. 'Anyone of interest going?' she asked.

'I doubt it.' Freddy looked at her sharply. 'Judith, you're just as bad as Megan. She said I looked like a princess and obviously expects the prince to turn up and complete the fairy-tale.'

Judith glanced at the clock. 'Aren't you going to be late?'

'The taxi's due in a minute. Judith,' Freddy was not to be deviated, 'you're always pointing out to your sixth-formers that Cinderella has a choice these days... that she doesn't have to try on the glass slipper, that there are other things in life instead of rushing into marriage just for security and the status quo.'

'I know I do,' replied Judith calmly, 'but Cinders hadn't any options, had she? She wasn't educated, poor thing, so there was no choice for her but to try on the slipper. There will be for my girls. I'm not against marriage, I'm *for* fulfilment. You've had your education and you've got somewhere with your life, doing what you want to do. You can afford to at least think about the slipper, and for all your independence I'd like to see you falling in love.'

'Oh, lor'!' groaned Freddy. 'Look, Ju, when I can find a man who will let me think and act for myself, who considers my job to be as important as his, who——' The front doorbell rang. '—treats me as an equal, who admits——'

'You'll be late, and there's no such paragon walking this earth,' interrupted Judith. 'You have to make do with the less than perfect.'

'—that women have a raw deal in climbing the professional ladder——' Freddy picked up her coat. '—and who is secure enough not to feel I'm a threat to his manhood, then, and only then, will I marry again.'

'We haven't built Utopia yet, and in the mean time you're going to have a lonely old age,' prophesied Judith and waved a dismissive hand. 'Go and wow 'em with the shoulder-pads, pal.'

Freddy grinned. The doorbell rang again and Megan shouted 'Doorbell!' from the bedroom. 'Don't forget to let Dini out,' reminded Freddy, and at the sound of his name the Boxer dog lying at Judith's feet lifted his black head and the stumpy tail wagged.

'If he finds another hole in the hedge I am not going hunting for him and that's final,' threatened Judith, glaring at the dog who looked back soulfully.

'You're an angel,' called Freddy as she rushed out of the room and into Megan's, giving her a hurried hug and a kiss, and flying out of the house.

The taxi driver, luckily, was not the talkative sort, and she sat lost in thought for the fifteen minutes it took to drive into the city centre. She knew she over-reacted sometimes with Megan, but bringing up a child as a single parent wasn't easy. Not that she had expected it to be, and she was luckier than most, having supportive parents and friends and a satisfying job. And she had a reasonable track record for her thirty-one years, she defended reflectively. It was true she had a failed marriage on the debit side, but that wasn't so terrible, was it? She had tried, really tried to make it work, but it hadn't come off. It wasn't often Freddy allowed herself to look back on that period, for no matter how hard she tried to kid herself, there were deep guilt feelings of failure within her that were not easy to live with.

But it was no good thinking negatively, she told herself firmly, gazing out of the window with unseeing eyes. She had some points on the credit side. Megan, for one, constantly delighting her, becoming each day more and more a person in her own right. It was a wonderful experience watching her grow and develop. As for occasional feelings of inadequacy, this was normal even in a two-parent family. Her job was enormously satisfying and she loved it. Freddy worked as a freelance producer-director for Atticus, an independent film company making dramas and documentaries for television. Openings were becoming more available for women in this field these days, but it was still an uphill drag, and dominated by men.

As for friends, she was not short of either sex. A divorcee, Freddy soon learned, was a target for men out for a good time, especially married men, but she was lucky to have a nucleus of supportive friends.

The taxi pulled up outside the hotel and the driver turned his head and said, 'We're here, lady, and cheer up, things can't be as bad as all that!'

Freddy realised she had been frowning, and laughed, saying as she alighted, 'You're right, they're not!'

She made her way into the hotel, taking the lift to the first floor, where the Atticus celebrations were being held. It was the company's fifteenth year and it had been decided to celebrate the fact, being a good opportunity to bring together clients and backers, writers and technicians, plus the Atticus work-force. By the sound of the noise coming from the reception room, the party was going with a swing.

Freddy squeezed her way through the crowd, smiling and saying hello, her tiredness lifting as she was caught up in the infectious gaiety, stopping at intervals to join in. It was the usual insular chit-chat that dominated such functions, a mixture of frivolous one-liners and earnest arguments, often amusingly malicious—bitchiness was not confined to women, Freddy had found.

'There you are, Freddy, my dear. I was hoping you'd make it.' Patrick Tyson, Executive Director of Productions and co-founder, with his wife, of

Atticus Productions, neatly scooped a glass of wine from the tray of a passing waiter and put it into her hand. He was blond, blue-eyed and handsome, astute and shrewd, and Freddy's boss.

'I wouldn't miss tonight for anything,' Freddy told him, smiling as she murmured her thanks for the wine. 'Everyone who's anyone is here, I see.'

A camera flashed and the photographer scribbled her name, offered by Patrick, and moved on.

'I doubt he's any wiser,' commented Freddy, laughing a little. 'He's thinking, Frederica Leigh? Never heard of her!'

'It takes time. Actors are the ones the viewers usually remember,' replied Patrick, his broad back shielding her from being jostled.

'I have an idea for *Sixty Minutes*, Patrick,' Freddy said and Patrick eyed her with approval.

'Good. Come and see me about it. How's *Tandy* going?'

'We're on schedule. I think this episode will be extra good.' *Tandy*, a police detective series, was an Atticus long-running success and Freddy was one of its producers. They spoke together for some minutes on matters concerning work and then Patrick left her.

Freddy continued her wandering, exchanging greetings with various Heads of Departments and representatives from the BBC and the IBA. It was obvious that speech-time was coming up, so she secured herself a good position so that she could see the top table where the Tysons were preparing to cut the cake. This was decorated with a television camera and the words 'Atticus—Fifteen Years' piped round the top. Glasses were being filled in readiness for the toasts, and conversation died down into a waiting silence as Patrick Tyson faced his guests.

'Ladies and gentlemen,' he began, 'Dinah and I welcome you all here this evening...'

Freddy listened for a while with her attention on the top table, and then her eyes roamed, watching the faces of those around her. As a child she had liked taking photographs, but as the years had passed she had come to realise that the moving picture excited her more. Freddy's camera eye was roving the sea of faces watching Patrick Tyson, judging which shots she would take if she were directing a programme right at this minute.

Still half listening to Patrick's speech, his words were pushed completely into the background as her eyes were caught and held by one particular face that now leaped into prominence out of the crowd.

My God! thought Freddy... Joe Corey! Her heart gave a painful jolt as the years backtracked and memories rushed in upon her. The recipient of this turbulent reaction was gazing thoughtfully at her, across the heads of fellow guests, as though she had been the object of his attention for some time. As their eyes met, Freddy went through a gamut of emotions in quick succession, shock and surprise making her face vulnerable for a few seconds. She was relieved when applause broke their contact and offered a good excuse for her to drag her eyes back to the Tysons, who were cutting the cake.

Patrick caught her eye, and his smile became personal and he tilted his glass to her. Freddy smilingly responded and thought, no candles on the cake, I must remember to tell Megan, grasping at something simple and ordinary. Cameras flashed from all sides and Freddy joined in the talk going on around her, presumably making sense, while she was wondering frantically why Joe Corey was here in Queensbridge.

She steeled herself to glance his way again and a queer feeling of isolation came upon her as she found herself once more the object of his attention. Her colour rose and she found her heart beating faster. His look was one familiar to her, managing to be both mocking and challenging. It used to make her wild, and she found it still did. He would be thoroughly enjoying himself, she thought grimly, and wished she had known he was to be here so that she could have prepared herself beforehand.

Her chin came up and she returned the stare with full measure. Joe lifted his glass in a travesty of Patrick's gesture of a few seconds before, a replay which Freddy coolly ignored. She watched him excuse himself from his companions—who she vaguely recognised as being connected with York-shire TV—and begin his journey across the space between them. He was halted now and then but not long detained, as it was obvious he was on his way somewhere. His eyes constantly kept her in check, gleaming cynically, as if aware of the possibility that she might disappear before he could get to her.

Did she want to run? Part of her did, part didn't, and with a bored, cool expression on her face she waited for him to reach her, feeling neither bored nor cool. With wry amusement she perceived the instant flowering in the women as he passed by. This was nothing new. There was something about Joe Corey that drew the female eye, all the more curious because he seemed nothing out of the ordinary to look at. Freddy had always wondered about meeting Joe again, and she had forgotten how the very air between them seemed to crackle and become charged with highly emotive vibes, putting her on the defensive immediately, the hairs on the back of her neck bristling.

'Well, well, well—if it isn't Joseph Corey Esquire, after all this time!' she said, her voice as steady as her gaze. 'What a surprise.'

Joe drawled, 'Frederica!' The hand she was holding out formally was ignored and she was drawn to him. His mouth found her lips slightly parted, astonishment at his audacity making them soft and vulnerable against his own. He drew back a little, smiling, murmuring, 'You taste of wine. Delicious.'

These days a kiss in public meant nothing, but Freddy knew that Joe had acted for the hell of it and she was furious, very conscious of curious eyes around them.

'Just what the hell are you doing, Joe Corey?' she hissed out of smiling lips.

'Greeting an old friend,' reproached Joe. 'Aren't you glad to see me, Fred?'

'As you see, I'm bowled over with excitement,' she replied with underlined sarcasm, adding, 'And don't call me Fred!' How easily the admonishment slipped out, just like the old days.

He grinned, eyes crinkling shrewdly as if he knew that despite the sarcasm there was a tiny fraction of her that was glad to see him, a bit of her that was rebelliously curious and intrigued. His eyes drifted over her. 'Still the same, and yet not quite,' he observed lazily. 'Frederica has grown up.'

'My God!' she answered tartly. 'So I should hope! What are you doing here, Joe?' His face went muzzy and she felt a little giddy and put out a hand to steady herself. 'I'm sorry, I think I shall have to sit down.'

Joe took the glass from her hand, commenting, 'You'd better lay off the booze.'

'I've only had two glasses!' Her vision had cleared suddenly, but she was still glad of his hand beneath her elbow.

'The waiters are doing an excellent job of topping up,' he told her drily. 'You've probably not noticed.'

'I think I'm hungry.'

'You women and your slimming fads!' Joe exclaimed in exasperation, changing direction towards the food.

'I'm not slimming,' Freddy ground out. 'I just haven't had time to eat much today, and I came late, and then the wine on an empty stomach...'

'I'd have thought,' Joe pointed out, filling a plate with food, 'that you were old enough to know better than to skip eating, Fred.'

'Thank you very much! I now feel a hundred—and *don't* call me Fred!'

He pushed the plate into her hand and cleared a space on the table. 'There doesn't appear to be a chair handy, but you can lean against me, if you like,' and he gave Freddy a malevolent smile. 'Or if that doesn't appeal, you can hitch yourself against this, it seems solid enough. Eat.' He watched her take the first mouthful.

A waiter came up and refilled Joe's glass, Freddy covered her own with the palm of her hand. She said, 'You didn't seem surprised to see me.'

'I thought you might be here. I knew you worked for Atticus, I've seen your name on their credits. I saw the *Sixty Minutes* documentary you did on handicapped children—I liked it very much.'

Freddy was glad she was eating. It gave her something to do. The programme as a whole had been very well reviewed, but Joe's praise sent a rush of pleasure through her out of all proportion, and it brought her up sharply. She said coolly, 'Thank you, I was quite pleased with it myself.'

'I always knew that determination such as yours would get somewhere,' Joe said reflectively. 'Talent and determination.'

She challenged his look. 'We were alike in those areas, weren't we?' This self-same ambition and drive had finally parted them—was he remembering that too, she wondered?

'I won a bet with myself, seeing you again,' Joe claimed, and Freddy eyed him warily. 'That you would turn out to be beautiful.'

She choked on a mouthful of fresh salmon, and suffered the ignominy of Joe pounding her on the back. When she had caught her breath Freddy said sarcastically, 'Very funny! You always did have peculiar ideas.'

His brows shot up. 'Beauty,' Joe drawled, 'is a fascinating subject, very individual. And you can admire a Chippendale chair, admit it has style and elegance, yet not wish to own it.'

Freddy bit savagely into a roll. Thank you very much, she muttered to herself. Let's not have a rush to the head, just because he's likened you to a chair!

Someone nearby made a remark to Joe and he half turned from her to answer. It was a good opportunity to covertly study him. He hadn't changed that much in the years since they had parted. His medium brown hair was still straight and thick, springing crisply at the new growth and expertly cut. He had a strong jaw, a nose his enemies called large, changeable brown eyes and a mouth that more often had a cynical curve at the corners, but which could break out into a devastating smile. No, Joseph Corey was no oil painting, but there was something about him, something that grew on you. Freddy had never been able to work it out.

'Feeling better?' Joe had turned back and caught her staring.

She put down the empty plate. 'I feel fine, that was delicious. Playing nursemaid isn't your usual style, Joe. Thanks.'

'I'm adaptable, and I didn't want you fainting all over me. What would folks have thought?'

'That the sight of you was too much for me? How quaint,' she mocked. 'And you never did tell me what brings you to Queensbridge.'

'I'm based here at the moment.' He surprised her by taking her left hand and studying the ringless

fingers, giving her a frowning look under his brows.
'I was told you were married.'

'I was. I am no longer. And you?' She took back
her hand and ignored the sharp awareness of
contact.

'No. You once told me I was a selfish, prejudiced
bastard, and I decided you were right and it wasn't
fair to subject any woman to be shackled to such
a poor specimen,' Joe replied, his voice and smile
decidedly sardonic.

Freddy felt a blush sweep all over her body and
her eyes were locked with his. She knew he was
remembering her saying those descriptive words
after they had made love, when Joe had asked her
to go with him to America and all hell had been
let loose. She had left the next day, and now they
had met up again, some seven, or was it eight years
later? Much water had flowed under the bridge since
then.

'Oh, good, you've found each other.' Patrick
Tyson's voice broke in on them and Freddy turned
to him gratefully. His wife was at his side and he
drew her forward, saying, 'Dinah, come and meet
Joseph Corey. Joe, my wife, Dinah.'

Dinah Tyson was a cool, poised woman, with
dark, perfectly groomed hair and an impeccable
manner. In the three years Freddy had known her
she had never seen Dinah lose her temper, nor show
spontaneous emotion of any kind. Dinah now
smiled graciously and extended her hand, saying,
'Mr Corey, I'm a fan of yours. I have all your books
and I loved *Wandering Man*. It fully deserved the
recognition it received. It's a pleasure to meet you.'

'How kind of you, Mrs Tyson,' replied Joe. 'May I congratulate you on your share of the company's fifteen years?'

Dinah received the compliment with another smile and then looked from Joe to Freddy, eyes piercing. 'You two know each other?' she asked.

Joe answered casually, 'We met some years back.' He tilted his head at Freddy. 'How long is it? Can you remember?'

Freddy could remember exactly, and knew Joe could, too. She could see him now, walking into the lecture-room, his notes in a folder under his arm and his eyes travelling round the class, hesitating slightly when they reached Freddy, the only female. She could even remember what he said, or very nearly, something like, 'We shall take chapter fifty-five of *Bleak House*, the section dealing with Lady Dedlock's meeting with Mr Guppy, and decide how we can turn it into a camera script.' Straight in and no messing for Joe Corey! He'd taught them twice a week, and for the full year's course Freddy had thought he disliked her—until it had ended, and she had found out differently.

She now shrugged and pretended to think. 'It must be ten years,' she replied, smiling slightly. Ten since they had met, eight since they had parted.

'You must have a great deal to talk over,' Dinah observed. 'Patrick, there are people waiting to say goodbye. I'm glad you've been persuaded to join our ranks, Mr Corey,' and allowing a smile to do for them both she drifted away.

Patrick, about to follow, turned back, saying, 'I've told Joe he can join you for a few days.

Freddy, to see how we work. Look after him, won't you?' He gave a quick smile. 'Goodnight, both.'

Freddy responded and then turned to Joe, who was watching her as if waiting for her reaction, his expression bland.

'I suppose I should have guessed,' she said, 'that you were here in a professional capacity.'

'Something could be in the offing in the future. Tyson's trying to drum up the money. It could come off, or not. Does that worry you, Fred, that I might be working for Atticus?'

'Why should it?' She glanced round the room.

'You give the impression of wanting to escape.'

'It's hardly worth escaping now if I've got you tagging along tomorrow, is it?'

'Exactly. Can I give you a lift?' He saw the hesitation on her face and added drily, 'Or get you a taxi?'

Brown eyes held green ones for some seconds and then Freddy said, 'Thank you, if it's not too much out of your way.' She mentioned the district in which she lived, learned that he would need to make only a slight detour and swung on her heel, walking ahead of him out of the room.

There were mirrors lining the corridor to the lift. Freddy glanced at their reflections, even now hardly able to believe that Joe Corey had come back into her life; she felt the same stabbing shock. The glistening red sequins caught the light, and her face looked brittle and unreal. Joe was walking with an easy, relaxed stride, half a pace behind her. Any man can look good in an evening suit, thought Freddy dourly, as they went down in the lift.

His car was a Sunbeam Tiger, brilliant red with gleaming chrome. Luckily the soft top was up. Freddy didn't care to be blown to pieces, and there was rain in the air. She remarked, 'You still like fast cars, Joe.'

He made no reply, waiting while she fixed her seat-belt. He started the engine and it rumbled into life, the merest touch of the accelerator bringing forth a subdued snarling roar. 'Perhaps you'd better refresh my memory on the best way to go,' Joe suggested, switching on the headlights, and Freddy complied.

The journey was taken in near silence, only Freddy's directions punctuating it. When the Tiger pulled up in Dean Close she said briskly, 'Thanks for the lift. About tomorrow—I'll meet you at the office, say eleven, if that's OK with you?'

'Eleven will be fine. Who do I ask for?'

'Sorry?' Freddy shot him a puzzled look.

'Your married name?' prompted Joe.

'Ask for Leigh. I've reverted to my maiden name.'

'Are you over it, Fred?'

Freddy couldn't fault his tone. She said matter-of-factly, 'Yes. It was a mistake for both of us. He has a new wife and she sounds a much better proposition.'

'And you?' Joe turned in his seat, leaning back against the door, resting an elbow on the steering wheel. The gold stud in his shirt cuff caught the light from the street-lamp as his hand lay across the leather trim. 'Have you a better proposition?'

'That's none of your damned business,' Freddy told him pleasantly.

'Why so uptight? I'm interested. We're old friends...'

'I am not uptight.'

'... and if you don't want to tell me, that's fine.' He glanced towards the house. The hall light was on, but elsewhere was in darkness. 'I just wondered if he was waiting up for you.'

Freddy expelled a deep breath. 'The only male in the house at the moment is a dog called Houdini, if you're so interested.'

'Very sensible. Deters burglars. Why Houdini?'

'Because he's always escaping. Joe, it's late. It's flattering that you should be so interested, but the last thing I want is you poking your big nose into my...'

'I know.' His voice was sympathetic. 'You have things all neat and tidy and along comes Corey to stir things up.'

'... life, and I have no intention of allowing you to stir ...'

'As for my nose, you shouldn't be personal, Fred. You know how sensitive I am about my nose.'

'You're a fine one to talk about being personal! And you know I didn't mean ...' Freddy stopped and gave an incredulous laugh. 'Sensitive? *You*? Joseph Corey, you're impossible!'

'No, no, merely curious. It's the writer in me.'

'Rubbish,' came back Freddy tartly, 'it's pure nosiness.'

He ran his forefinger down the bridge of his nose. 'There you go again.' Pain was in his voice, changing to satisfaction as he added, 'You nearly smiled that time.' He peered into her face. 'I was beginning to think that the old Fred had completely disappeared under all this welter of sophistication. Very smart. I wholeheartedly approve.'

'I can't tell you how glad that makes me,' Freddy answered with mild sarcasm, 'and *don't* call me *Fred*!' She saw the flash of a smile, and her hand was taken in his and he studied her palm.

'Do you believe in fate?' he asked lazily.

Freddy looked at him askance, conscious of the feel of his pulse against the palm of her hand. 'I don't know. Yes, I suppose so.' She pulled her hand free, making the excuse of tucking a fall of hair from her eyes. 'Do you?'

There was a knowing glint in his eyes as if he had guessed exactly the reasons for breaking contact. 'Yes,' he replied promptly, not needing to give the matter thought, 'although I'm arrogant enough to want to be in charge of my own destiny. Fate opens doors, offers paths—I rather think it's up to us whether we close the door or walk the path.' He leaned across to push down the doorhandle and it swung open. Freddy could feel the warmth of his breath on her cheek, he was so close. She stiffened, expecting a kiss, not knowing whether she wanted one or not. And then he moved away, saying cheerfully, 'Goodnight, Frederica,' and she was out of the car, forcing herself to walk without haste up the path.

She didn't look back as she let herself in, and heard the sound of the engine opening up as the Tiger moved off. She stood for a moment, carefully thinking of nothing in particular. Houdini padded into the hall and pushed his blunted nose into the palm of her unresisting hand, wanting to be noticed. She absently scratched his head and went to look in on Megan.

The child was breathing lightly, two red patches on her cheeks, a disreputable rabbit clutched in one hand. Freddy stood looking down on her and, as if she sensed her mother's presence, Megan's eyes flickered open and she stirred. Freddy stood still, not wanting to disturb her so that she woke fully.

Megan murmured sleepily, 'Did he come?'

'Yes, he came,' Freddy replied softly, taking the easy answer, intent on soothing the child back to sleep.

'Good,' said Megan, and turned over.

# CHAPTER TWO

'How did your evening go?' asked Judith the next morning, joining Freddy and Megan for breakfast.

'He came,' Megan told her importantly, lifting her head from a glass of milk and presenting a white upper lip.

'Darling,' broke in Freddy quickly, 'you were half-asleep last night, so I didn't explain properly. It wasn't Indiana Jones, but an old friend who turned up.' She gave her daughter a comical shrug and a grimace. 'I reckon we'll have to make do with the poster.'

Megan copied both the gesture and the grimace, asked if she could get down, was told to go and wash her face and left the room. Judith murmured, 'That child I can see ending up on the stage.'

Freddy answered without heat, 'God forbid!'

She poured a cup of tea and passed it over. Then she dropped two slices of bread into the toaster and turned to glance out of the window. The kitchen was her favourite room, not because it was elegant, for it was quite the reverse. The house had been built in the early part of the century and still retained old-fashioned cupboards and quarry tiles. But the kitchen faced the garden, where Houdini was now mooching about, and she could see splashes of purple and white from the Michaelmas daisies, and red and gold from the dahlias. Late roses were climbing the dividing wall, and signs of autumn showed in the turning colours of the trees.

Judith could contain her curiosity no longer. 'Am I allowed to ask who this old friend is?' she enquired.

'A fellow I knew years ago,' replied Freddy, 'by the name of Joseph Corey. Just look at that rose, Judith, the pink one—it's so perfect it hardly looks real.'

'The name's vaguely familiar,' remarked her friend, uninterested in nature just at that moment.

'You borrowed one of his books some time back, and enjoyed it if I remember rightly. *Wandering Man*, it's called. Him.'

'Really? You didn't say you knew him personally,' protested Judith.

'No, well...' Freddy rescued the toast as it popped up '...I guess I didn't see any point.'

Judith stared. 'Is that all? Ah, come on, Freddy! How friendly is this old friend? A real live author, for God's sake!'

Freddy laughed. 'It was a long time ago, Judith, when I knew him. He was one of the lecturers on the TV course.'

'Oh, old,' pouted Judith, disappointed.

'No, he was about twenty-seven then. He was a good teacher.' Freddy began to butter the toast.

'What did he lecture?' Judith sensed a need for Freddy to talk, and was quite happy to encourage her.

'Scripts and adaptations of novels...how to use the camera to move the plot along visually, that sort of thing.'

'And he wrote books as well?' marvelled Judith, spreading her toast with marmalade and eyeing the clock.

'He was drawn into television when one of his books was made into a play.'

'Some people's energy is positively disgusting,' pronounced Judith. 'What's he like—to look at, I mean?'

Freddy reached and took up a book that was lying on the nearby cupboard, handing it to Judith. Judith looked at the photograph on the back cover, making no comment on the fact that the book was so handy, and asked, 'What's he doing in Queensbridge?'

'Probably going to work for Atticus. I doubt he'll be staying long . . . wandering man would be a good name for Joe Corey.'

'Am I allowed to ask if you were pleased to see him?'

'You could say I had mixed feelings,' Freddy replied drily, 'and you can remove that too innocent look! You're right, we were more than *just good friends*,' putting the last three words into mocking italics. 'In fact, we had one hell of a time together, lasting nearly a year.'

Eyes wide with interest, Judith studied the photograph again. 'He looks as though he could be fun. Why? I mean, why only a year?'

'We were too much alike and had too much to do,' stated Freddy. She poured herself another cup of tea and offered the pot to Judith, her eyes drawn to the photograph. 'Joe had the chance to go to Hollywood to work on a film script. He wanted me to go with him. Just like that. Drop everything and go with him.' She gave a laugh and shook her head, remembering. 'I'd just started my first job—which I'd been darned lucky to get, I might add—and he was taking it for granted I'd give up this fantastic chance. We had a row to end all rows and I told him he'd hate Hollywood, that it wasn't his scene, and he said how could he know unless he tried it— which was quite true and Joe was all for trying everything—oh, and lots more, plus the ''I thought you loved me'' scenario. All the corny stuff delivered with fury and passion.'

'Did you love him?'

'Yes, I loved him, but not enough to blow the chances of my career. I remember I suggested that if he loved me he would give Hollywood up. I didn't expect him to, of course, but he got the point . . . it was all right for me to trot along in his wake. I told him he only wanted someone to bask in the shadows of his own ego and that there would be plenty who would, no doubt, jump at the opportunity.'

'And were there?'

'I imagine so.'

'Why didn't you keep in touch? Why did it have to be such a complete break?'

'Pride, I suppose. We'd both said too much. Maybe if I'd gone about it differently things wouldn't have exploded like they did, but I was battling against male egos all day at work, and the one person who I thought would understand my difficulties and be sympathetic let me down. I doubt Joe had given it much thought. He was off to

America and wanted me with him. Quite simple. He only stayed over there to do that one film.'

'Is he married these days?'

'These days?' Freddy grinned. 'You can tell from his books that he has a nice line in cynicism on that particular subject.'

'So how do you feel about him now?' asked Judith.

Freddy gave her a suspicious look. 'What do you mean?'

'Simple question. You meet the guy again after a break of a few years. When you looked into his eyes, what did you feel?'

'Credit me with some sense, Ju!' protested Freddy. 'You don't put your fingers in the fire twice unless you're a complete idiot. I got burned rather badly once.'

'No need to put your hand right in, is there? A little scorching could be fun. You've got in a rut emotionally. Treat yourself.' Judith scraped back her chair, gulped down the rest of the tea and disappeared into the hall, calling, 'Meggie, it's time we were off,' coming back in to add, 'You have to decide whether to live dangerously or vegetate.'

'Isn't there a happy medium?' demanded Freddy wryly.

The first thing Freddy did, after waving Judith's Mini out of sight, was to replace Joe's book on the shelf. She avoided looking at the photograph; she didn't need reminding of the level stare and quirky mouth. Meeting Joe again had set her brain into high-speed activity last night and, when she had tossed and turned and finally realised she was not going to get off to sleep, she had fetched the book and skimmed through it again. It was well written, with humour and soul-searching self-analysis, giving a slightly cynical view of life, but ending on an upward note. It had been nominated for the Booker Prize.

Freddy was unable to dispel Joe from her mind while she went around doing the household chores. He had been closer to the truth than she cared to admit when he had joked about her life being neat and tidy. And what was wrong with that? It had taken time and discipline to make it so, and she couldn't exist as a single parent with it otherwise. Corey, she decided firmly, could stay out of it.

Freddy gazed out of the window, hands in washing-up water. Wasn't she assuming rather a lot? Meeting trouble half-way? Joe had been very Joe-like last night, a mood she knew well, but in the clear light of day, who was Freddy Leigh, other than an ex-lover?

Live dangerously or vegetate. Judith's words rang in her ears. Freddy had no intention of doing either. Things never stayed the same, she was realistic enough to accept that. Judith would marry her biochemist and leave, and Mrs Mallory, Freddy's stalwart, dependable daily, would decide to retire. Such things were out of her control and she would adapt accordingly, but Joe Corey was something she could have a say in. Freddy wrote a note to Mrs Mallory, reminding her to collect Megan from school at the usual time, and then drove the Renault into the city for an hour's session in the library where she did some research on an idea for a programme.

As she made her way to the Atticus offices her thoughts returned to Joe. He had been hovering on the edge of them while she had been in the library, much to her annoyance, and now that they were about to meet again Freddy was determined to treat him just like any other professional colleague. She had barely taken off her coat when the telephone rang and the girl from reception said, 'A Mr Corey is here to see you, Miss Leigh.' There was an archness in her voice that told Freddy how quickly news of the night before's kiss had travelled, quicker than most, for she hugged her private life closely and no one knew much about it. She said briskly, 'I'll come on down.'

She made her way to reception and was determined there would be no welcoming kiss this time. Joe was reading a newspaper left for visitors' use which he folded and dropped when he saw her.

'Good morning, Joe,' Freddy said briskly. 'I have to wait for a telephone call, but it shouldn't be long. I thought you might like to see round while we're waiting.' She looked beyond him to reception and the two girls behind the desk hastily averted their eyes and became busy. Freddy subdued a smile of satisfaction and turned, leading the way into a corridor off. As they passed each door she listed the occupants.

'Administrative Manager, Head of Scripts and Development, Director of Productions—that's Patrick Tyson, of course—plus their secretaries' rooms.' The lift doors were already open and she stepped in, waiting until Joe joined her, and then pressed the button.

Now she was obliged to look at him fully. He was leaning against the opposite wall, offering a more casual image than the night before, with a tweed jacket, check shirt, a mustard tie and brown cords. Wrapped once round his neck and hanging nearly to his knees was a hand-knitted vermilion-coloured scarf.

'I see,' he drawled, giving a lazy smile, 'that you're admiring my scarf.'

'I was thinking I might have to put on dark glasses,' admitted Freddy.

'A labour of love by a favourite niece.' Joe lifted up an end, giving it due attention. 'She was worried about the mistakes, but I told her they made the thing unique, that someone who doesn't make a mistake makes nothing.'

'Very true,' agreed Freddy, knowing all about mistakes from experience. 'I didn't know you had a niece, Joe.'

'No reason why you should. I have three, as a matter of fact. I can't remember us being much interested in anyone other than ourselves, can you, Fred?' His eyes held hers mockingly.

The lift stopped and the doors slid open. Freddy made no reply and stepped out, looking back when Joe didn't follow.

'No mistakes in that,' he commented, eyes drifting over the grey-green knitted two-piece she was wearing. He pushed himself from the wall and strolled out of the lift.

'I should hope not, at the price,' observed Freddy crisply, immediately self-conscious about her body and making a great effort to walk naturally. 'On this floor we have the Casting, Projection and Editing rooms, and this, and the room beyond, are for freelance. The floor above has a couple of interview rooms and houses the commercial section.' She opened the nearest door and walked into a room consisting of four large desks and numerous cupboards. The air was stale and Freddy emptied a couple of used ashtrays and opened a window.

'We should have the place to ourselves for a bit,' she said, making the window-catch firm. 'Would you like coffee? It's always on the go. No milk, I'm afraid.' She collected two cups and crossed to the coffee-maker.

'Do you prefer being freelance?' Joe hitched himself on to one of the desks and Freddy handed him his coffee and set down the sugar-bowl in front of him. She went to another desk and sat down in the chair behind it.

'It suits me. There's a tendency to get stuck with either drama or documentary when you're working for the bigger corporations. You get labelled. Here there's more choice. Patrick is accommodating that way.'

'You like working for him?'

'Yes . . . I owe him a lot. He took rather a chance on me initially.' The telephone rang and Freddy answered it. It didn't take long and she made notes in her diary and when the call was finished she downed her coffee and rose. 'We can go now, if you're ready.' She unhooked her coat from the back of the chair, waited while Joe finished his drink and then led the way back to reception. She told the girls there where she would be in case she was wanted—this in case Megan had an accident, or was ill—and joined Joe who was waiting outside on the steps of the building.

Well, that had gone off all right, Freddy thought as she buttoned up her coat. A light breeze caught and tossed a heap of leaves that had settled round the base of one of the trees that lined the pavement. It had been September when she and Joe had first met, she remembered.

'Shall we go in my car? There's no point in taking two, unless you have to shoot off fairly soon?' Freddy wondered if she sounded too hopeful.

'I'm completely in your hands,' replied Joe expansively, 'and becoming more and more impressed with the efficient Miss Leigh every minute.'

'Good. You might tell Patrick.'

'I doubt he needs telling. Patrick, if nothing else, is astute.'

'Don't you like him?' There had been an odd nuance in his voice that prompted the question, glancing back over her shoulder as she asked it.

'I don't care for him as a person too much.' Joe grabbed her arm and swung her out of the path of a woman with a pram. For a few seconds Freddy was hard against his chest, breathing in the smell of him, feeling the strength of his hands. She muttered 'Thanks' as she regained her balance, aware that her heart was beating that much faster. Perhaps Judith was right; she *was* in an emotional rut—poor old sex-starved Freddy, she mocked—but Joe Corey wasn't the answer.

As she opened up the Renault, Houdini rose from the depths of the rear and attempted to get through to the front. 'Back, Dini,' she ordered, and he compromised by getting stuck between the two seats. She slid behind the wheel, pushing his head away, and leaned over to unlock the passenger door, saying as Joe joined her, 'He's quite tame, don't worry.'

'I'm very glad to hear it.' There was laughter in his voice. 'Your chaperon, Fred?'

She grinned. 'Hardly. He looks ferocious, but he's the daftest dog imaginable,' and to prove it, Houdini pushed his black face inquisitively into Joe's and proceeded to give it a loving scrub with an over-active tongue. With the ease of someone well used to dogs and their behaviour Joe thrust him off good-naturedly and dried himself with the end of his scarf.

'I usually leave him at home,' Freddy explained, 'but my daily isn't coming in until after midday, and he looked so sad . . . He's a mournful-looking beast at the best of times, but when he really tries it's devastating emotional blackmail. Have you no dignity, Dini?' she demanded severely, bursting into laughter at the sight of four legs waving in the air as he rolled on his back on the seat for Joe to scratch him. She turned to Joe, ready to share her enjoyment, the laughter fading as she found him watching her with an odd look on his face. She asked uncertainly, 'What's the matter?'

'I've just had my first glimpse of the Frederica I used to know. Are you on your guard against everyone, Fred, or is it only me?'

A pulse beat rapidly in her throat. She gave a dismissive laugh and started up the engine. 'I'm not the same person you knew, Joe, so it's no good looking for her.' She drove out of the car park, changing the subject by saying, 'I'm taking you to look in on a *Tandy* shoot. Have you seen any of the series?'

Joe was silent a moment, as if he were contemplating challenging the switch of conversation. Finally he replied, 'I've seen one or two.'

'The clients think it will take another twelve episodes and so far the scripts uphold their view. There's a team of writers so perhaps it's easier for the scripts to remain fresh, less chance of them becoming boring. Each episode takes eight and a half weeks, and it's shot on a tight budget. We're lucky to have David Herrick working on this episode—there's a team of directors and producers as well as writers on *Tandy*.' Freddy pulled into a side street and parked behind a row of cars. 'We're here,' she offered, and, ignoring Houdini's reproachful face, led the way into a large building that ran the length of the street. The red light above the inner doors wasn't on, but Freddy still waited, watching through the glass until the scene being rehearsed finished before they entered. It was as if they had walked into the interior of a real police station, only the cameras and lights indicating that it was a television studio.

Freddy and Joe positioned themselves out of sight of the cameras and waited for the scene to be shot. When it was finished and the director went into a huddle with his lighting cameraman, Freddy explained, 'This is a permanent set with room at the back to build a couple of temporary ones. As you see, we use a four-man camera crew and we hire all the equipment—it's more economical in the long run, we've found. They're making technical improvements all the time, so it means we're always using the most up-to-date equipment.' She finished speaking as a grey-eyed, dark-haired man in his early forties came up, a warm smile lighting up his face.

'Hello, Freddy, glad you've come, I wanted a word with you. How were yesterday's rushes?'

'Fine, David. You'll be pleased with them.' She glanced at Joe, adding, 'Patrick hoped you wouldn't mind if I brought Joe Corey along with me this morning—he's interested in the way we work.'

She made the introductions and Joe asked a few pertinent questions, indicating he was no novice on a television set, and then he said, 'I'm sure you have things to discuss,' and he excused himself and wandered over to the camera crew, the head cameraman shaking his hand enthusiastically as if he knew him. Freddy was reminded that however popular Joe was with the ladies he was also well liked by men. She also remembered how they could never go anywhere without Joe bumping into someone he knew, and he hadn't changed in that respect, either.

'Who is he?' David asked, curiously. 'The name's vaguely familiar. Should I know him?'

'Mm... I think so. Do you remember a play set in Flanders during the First World War called *Over The Hill*? It was based on one of his books.' She glanced over at Joe.

'Ah, yes, that fellow. An impressive play.' David fell silent, following her gaze, adding after a moment, 'What's he like?'

'Easy enough to drag around,' Freddy answered evasively. 'Are we still having dinner together next Friday? If so, can you come to me? I might have sitter problems.'

David gave his slow smile and tucked her arm through his. 'Yes, we are, and yes, I'll come. I'll bring the wine. Eight o'clock all right?'

Freddy smiled and nodded, and they began to walk over to the crew. She had known David for as long as she had worked for Atticus. He was a widower with two young teenage sons at boarding school. She found him an undemanding, understanding companion and respected his work. They often found themselves paired together professionally. As they neared, Joe turned his head and watched them approach, his eyes coolly assessing, his expression impassive.

'We'll break for lunch now,' David said, looking at his watch. 'Are you coming over?' he asked Freddy, who glanced at Joe.

'Does a pub lunch suit you, Joe?' she asked, and when he said that it did, the whole of the cast and crew made their way over the road to the Crossed Keys public house.

Nothing of note happened during lunch. Freddy and David discussed the rest of the week's schedule, while bursts of laughter issued from the group around Joe. He was listening to his cameraman friend with a smile on his face and an expression of one who is hearing anecdotes about himself. David shook Joe's hand before he left, calling back to Freddy, 'See you Friday,' as he went out of the door.

Joe made no comment, his eyes following David's progress through the window until he disappeared into the studio's entrance.

Freddy checked the time and said, 'I'm doing a follow-up on a nose job next and meeting the crew in thirty minutes. If you're ready, I think we'd better go.'

'Plastic surgery, do you mean?' queried Joe as they stepped out of the pub. Freddy nodded, digging into her bag for the car keys. Houdini, who had been given a walk before lunch, was breathing heavily on the side window, steaming the glass. 'It's for the *Sixty Minutes* documentary programme. She's quite a character, Viv. Good fun and...' Freddy's voice trailed and she frowned, hunting in the pockets of her coat, and again in her bag, finally peering through the window at the keys dangling tantalisingly out of reach from the steering column lock. She closed her eyes, gave a huge sigh and said flatly, 'I've locked us out.' She glanced at Joe, face blank, and then at the keys, disbelief colouring her voice although she could see the evidence all too clearly as she said again, 'I've locked us out!'

'So it would seem,' replied Joe, controlling his amusement. 'No set of spares?'

Freddy dived into her bag again and stopped, an arrested expression on her face. 'I changed my bag in a hurry this morning.' She glared at him. 'I've never done this before—and don't you dare laugh, Joe Corey.'

'I wouldn't dream of doing so.'

'What the hell do I do now?' Freddy hurriedly looked at her watch.

'Wait,' said Joe laconically, 'all may not be lost.' He returned to the Crossed Keys, coming back with a screwdriver and a wire coat-hanger. 'Just one of my many accomplishments,' he confided and set to work, gently prising down the window enough to insert the hanger—now bent to suit the purpose— and, after some delicate probing, teasing up the lock.

Expelling a long held-in breath, Freddy exclaimed, 'Joe, you're a bloomin' marvel!' Opening the door with relief, she quietened Houdini, who had become wildly excited by the whole affair, slobbering over everything, and settled in her seat.

'Glad to be of service, ma'am,' Joe said, smiling a little wickedly. He returned the screwdriver to the landlord and tossed the ruined hanger on to the back window-ledge.

Freddy set off, anxiously looking at the dash clock. 'Today is our final session,' she explained. 'Viv is twenty-five and we've followed her through the initial visit to her doctor and from there to the consultant surgeon. I personally can't see that much difference between the old nose and the new one—

he removed a piece of bone from the bridge—but Viv's delighted and that's all that matters. We covered the operation, monitored the swelling and bruising, and now her face is back to normal we're ready to film the nose in all its perfection. It's taken about nine weeks from the op to now.' She swung the car into a cul-de-sac and pulled up behind an Atticus van. 'The crew's here, but we're not late—thanks to you.'

As she introduced Joe to Viv and the crew, Freddy silently prayed that nothing else would go wrong. She had the most understandable wish for a smooth final session, with Joe looking on, and to her relief everything progressed without any further hitches. When she was satisfied with the takes the crew dismantled the camera, lights and microphone and left. As Freddy and Joe were about to leave, a cup of coffee later, Freddy promised Viv that she would let her know the date the programme was going out.

As they approached the Renault Freddy had the most awful feeling sweep over her, and she stopped hard in her tracks. Joe, a pace behind, nearly bumped into her.

'What's the matter?' he asked, puzzled, glancing at her horror-stricken face and then following her gaze, enlightenment dawning. Freddy went slowly up to the car, looked in, and then turned to him.

'I have never ever done this before,' she said slowly and distinctively, 'You can laugh, Joe, but I just can't believe it!' And then she was laughing too, rattling the door-handle hopefully. 'Perhaps you'd go and ask Viv if I can borrow the necessary tools?'

Controlling himself with an effort, Joe went back into the house. On his return Freddy held out her hand, saying grimly, 'I might as well learn how to do it myself.'

Houdini needed to be calmed once more, the second bent hanger joined the first and the screwdriver was returned to an amused Viv. Freddy was grateful that the crew had already left; she would never have lived it down.

On the whole, the day had gone remarkably well, she thought, pleased, apart from the totally demoralising farce of the car keys, of course. Just thinking of that made her want to gnash her teeth— oh, how she had wanted everything to go smoothly this day of all days! Yet it had been funny! And Joe had been very sweet. Her lips curved at the corners; she glanced his way and her breath caught in her throat. It ought not to be allowed, she decided grimly, such smiles as Joe Corey could produce, right out of the blue, without the hint of mockery in them. It was unnerving.

'Do you know the Queen's Theatre?' she asked, and pointed to the red brick building coming up on their right. 'Awful architecture, in my opinion, but it has a terrific reputation professionally.'

'So I understand.' Joe glanced across as they drove by. 'Do you go?'

Freddy sounded shocked. 'Of course I go! Have to support the local theatre.'

'And the artistic director, Adam Carlyon, do you know him?'

Freddy nodded. 'His son, Michael, goes to...' The same school as my daughter, Megan, was what she was going to say, but before she could work out the reasons she had changed it to ' ... our local school,' with barely a pause in the flow of words.

'Have you booked to see the new John Bennett play, *Choices*, yet?'

'No, I must do so, his plays are always popular.'

'How about coming with me? I have two tickets for the twenty-fifth of next month.'

Freddy shot him a blank look, her wits deserting her in surprise, and guided the car into the Atticus car park, pulling to a halt alongside the gleaming red Tiger. In the silence when the engine stopped she was without a single excuse, her brain empty. She asked bluntly, 'Why me?'

His lips turned down in sardonic amusement. 'How suspicious you sound, Fred. Why not you? If you want reasons, I can give you some. It's a way of saying thank you for putting up with me over the next few days—I'm sure it was the last thing you wanted. I'd sooner take someone than go by myself, and I don't know anyone else to ask.'

'I don't believe that,' Freddy challenged drily.

'And the idea has occurred that you might feel like humouring me.' Joe glanced back to the rear shelf where the two bent coat-hangers lay.

'That sounds suspiciously like blackmail,' protested Freddy mildly. She watched him put an arm across the seat and smooth his hand over Houdini's domelike head. She thought that was something Joe did well—knowing when to bide his time. He had enormous energy and drive, but had also the instinct of knowing when to curb it. She took the diary from her bag and flipped the pages until she came to the date she was seeking. There was nothing down for that particular Saturday, and there was enough time to arrange for Megan.

It would be wise to make an excuse...

'If we could come to some mutual agreement,' she murmured, turning to look at him, feeling a spark of anticipation stirring inside. They were playing games, and it seemed a long time since she had allowed herself that indulgence.

Joe drawled, 'Oh, I'm sure we can work something out between us!' Laughter was pulling at his mouth and lighting up his brown eyes.

'Well,' the word was long drawn out, 'my reputation is at stake. I've built up a name for efficiency here at Atticus which I'm loath to forfeit, but if you promise *never* to breathe a word about the coat-hanger and screwdriver...'

'Two,' corrected Joe gently.

'Two coat-hangers and screwdrivers,' repeated Freddy with dignity, 'then I'd be delighted to take the other ticket off your hands.' She quite spoilt the effect by bursting into laughter.

'It's a deal,' he confirmed, and held out his hand. Freddy's went into it and recognition shot through her. Her hand seemed quite content to remain where it was, but enough was enough. She pulled gently and was free. Joe swung himself from the car and, turning, bent his body to peer back in.

'Much the best thing to keep quiet about it,' he agreed kindly, 'or folk might be wondering why I have such a traumatic effect on you, Frederica... if you've never done such a thing before.' His brows rose provocatively and he shut the door.

Driving home, Freddy informed Houdini more than once that she wanted her head examined.

Frederica. No one could say her name quite like Joe.

# CHAPTER THREE

LOOKING back, some weeks later, Freddy smiled ruefully at how jumpy she had been when Joe had first turned up, for, apart from that disastrous day when all she had seemed to do was lock herself out of the car, the following few days when he'd joined her on her work schedule were totally unremarkable. She had decided to be pleasant but distanced with him, and when Joe made no attempt to challenge this stance she felt a ridiculous sense of being let down. She subsequently bumped into him a number of times around town and at Atticus, and sighted him having lunch in her favourite restaurant, a young and attractive strawberry-blonde hanging on to his arm like a limpet. This was no surprise. Joe Corey without a female in tow, and a good-looking one at that, was difficult to imagine.

One evening in late October Freddy arrived home to find Megan playing happily with a friend, and Mrs Mallory, Freddy's housekeeper, putting the finishing touches to the evening meal. When Mrs Mallory had left, Freddy joined the children in a board game entailing much giggling and a little cheating before taking the friend home, four doors down. This was an important time of the day for Freddy, and as often as she was able she liked to share it with Megan, eating together, Megan chatting about her day at school and any worries she might have.

After settling her daughter for sleep, Freddy rang her parents, confirming that she hoped to be spending some time with them in Boston for Christmas. She had just settled down with a book when Judith arrived home, singing the praises of *Choices*, the play currently on at the Queen's Theatre, which she had just been to see.

'You'll enjoy it,' she told Freddy, pouring two measures from the bottle she had brought in with her. 'And I've found out what's tempted Joseph Corey to Queensbridge.' She passed one of the glasses to Freddy and took the other glass and herself to the other large, comfortable armchair, kicking off her shoes and tucking up her legs. She took a sip of the drink and fished a brochure out of the pocket of her skirt. '*Voilà*! The spring and summer programme is advertised, and lo and behold, one of the forthcoming plays is being directed by Joseph Corey. There's a bit about him, listing his credits, finishing with the information that he's currently writing a book. How about that, then?'

She tossed the brochure over to Freddy who closed her book and scanned the contents. The play was Shakespeare's *Othello*, which was being produced the following May and going out on tour in June.

'So his sojourn here is not to be a brief one,' commented Judith, her eyes resting speculatively on her friend over the rim of her glass. 'How is he these days? You don't talk about him much.'

'Simply because I rarely see him,' Freddy replied calmly. 'He's in America at the moment.'

'But I thought he was taking you to see *Choices* on Saturday?'

'And he is. There are such things as machines that fly, Judith.'

'Ha-very-ha.' Judith decided she wasn't going to get anything more on the subject of Joe Corey and changed the subject.

The Queen's brochure made a handy bookmark and, when Freddy decided to read for a while before going to sleep, she found herself browsing through the brochure instead. *Othello* in May, touring in June... Joe would be here through winter, spring and summer. She hardly knew how she felt about the news, but then, Freddy couldn't understand herself half the time these days.

At the office the following day she found a short letter from Joe waiting for her, penned in his thin, scrawling writing, telling her that he would pick her up on the Saturday evening, naming a time. Judith was away that weekend, so Freddy arranged for Megan to sleep at the house of her nearby playmate. It was a reciprocal arrangement and Megan was highly delighted.

Getting ready that evening became a farce. Freddy had decided what she was going to wear and had a lazy soak in the bath, washing her hair and generally pampering herself. She wandered round in bra, panties and stockings, leisurely making-up and then, when the time came to put on the dress she had picked out, she decided against it. Half an hour later her bed was strewn with articles that had been tried on and thrown off. When the doorbell rang she whipped round and stared in horror at the clock, seized a silk dressing-gown and hurriedly thrust it on and went to answer the door.

She had to hold back Houdini, who wanted to make his own boisterous greeting. Joe stepped inside and Freddy clutched the robe fronts together, Houdini's gyrations proving too much for the hastily tied belt.

'Hello, Joe,' she said breathlessly, taking in the grey suit, the red tie and matching handkerchief in the top pocket, the white and red finely striped shirt. Glory! He did look gorgeous! Her eyes lifted to his face and she found him just the same—warm brown eyes, quirky mouth, a little tired-looking.

'I'm sorry, Joe, I shan't be a minute. Go on in, will you?' Freddy escaped into her bedroom, furious with herself. Where was the cool, poised image she had wanted to present? She grabbed the dress she had first chosen and threw it on in haste. It was a silk jersey, soft and fine, in a shade the fashion world called peppermint. It was graceful and flowing, with long sleeves and a front cross-over in draped folds, the hem coming to below the knee. She stared at herself in the mirror, remembering the picture she had presented at the door, and hoped that this would be an improvement. There wasn't time to mess about. Freddy pushed her feet into black patent shoes, sprayed herself with Van Cleef's *First*, pulled despairingly at a few straggling loose tendrils and decided she would have to do.

She joined Joe in the sitting-room, and said in a vexed voice, 'Oh, Joe, I should have offered you a drink! I'm sorry. Will you have one now?'

'Thanks, no. And don't worry, I've been catching up on the evening news.' He returned the paper to where he had found it, and his eyes drifted appreciatively over her. 'Shall we go? We might have trouble parking.' He helped her on with her coat, a soft wool in oatmeal, and followed her to the door. Before opening it, he asked lazily, 'Missed me, Fred?' and an eyebrow rose extravagantly.

The warmth of approval in his eyes when she had walked into the room had sent Freddy's spirits spiralling, but she was determined not to show it. 'Why, Joe, haven't you been around?' she asked, eyes wide. 'I hadn't noticed.'

With his sardonic features showing faint amusement he made no comment, the lids dropping over his eyes so that they were nearly, but not quite, closed. Freddy found herself having to use all her reserves to out-stare him, and as she followed him out to the Tiger she wondered who had won that round.

The Queen's Theatre had a festive air about the place that was indicative of a successful run. The bars on both floors were a moving mass of people, giving out a steady level of noise. Joe disappeared, saying he was going to order interval drinks, and Freddy caught sight of the theatre's artistic director's wife, Elizabeth Carlyon, threading her way towards her through the crowd.

Their knowledge of each other was merely from meeting at the school gates and an occasional school function, but, even from this minimal contact, each instinctively liked the other and secretly wanted to further the acquaintance.

Liz Carlyon was a year older than Freddy, with friendly blue eyes and a warm, outgoing personality. 'Hello! Freddy Leigh, isn't it?' she exclaimed, smiling, as she came up. 'I was so pleased when I learned you were with Joe tonight. We're all sitting together! Where *is* Joe? Oh, there he is, talking to Adam. It's been such a rush getting here in time! I start off with plenty to spare, and then something always throws me out—usually the children.' She grinned. 'The best way is for Adam to put the clocks forward twenty minutes, which works quite well.'

The first bell summoning the audience to their seats brought Joe and Adam to their side. Adam shook Freddy's hand, his manner more reserved than his wife's, but showing kindly interest. He was tall, with cool grey eyes and dark hair silvering at the temples, giving his attractive, aquiline features an authoritative air. As talk progressed it became obvious that Joe was a friend as well as a colleague and, listening to the Carlyons together, watching the exchange of glances, Freddy felt a sharp pain shoot through her. She squashed it immediately, for she was ashamed of it—envy was a bitter rue to carry around and could eat away the soul... and in any event, her life was extremely fulfilling, and she did have Megan. Joe caught her eye and gave her the suggestion of a wink and the pain went completely. Megan, satisfying work and friends—what more could she want?

The second bell sounded and they made for their seats. As the play unfolded Joe's strawberry-blonde came on to the stage. Her name, according to the programme, was Nina Welsh.

'Oh, dear!' gasped Liz, laughing. 'What a wickedly funny play! Nina really is extraordinarily beautiful, isn't she?'

Freddy agreed. The play finished to strong applause, and afterwards the cast of six joined them in the bar and received well-earned congratulations. Nina Welsh turned out to have an even more stunning effect offstage. Her hair would always draw the eye, but she had the most astonishing pansy-mauve eyes. Young, pretty and talented about summed up Nina Welsh, thought Freddy.

A table had been reserved at a nearby Italian restaurant and Freddy found that she and Joe were included in the party. She was seated between Adam and one of the actors in the play, with Joe sitting opposite between Liz and Nina. As he stretched out to pour wine into Freddy's glass Joe smiled—a wide, warm, intimate smile that caused Freddy's heart to leap into her throat and her stomach to make a sickening lurch. Her expression must have shown something unusual, for his look was arrested and his eyebrows rose as he searched her face, the wine bottle suspended.

Nina called out gaily for his attention, holding up her empty glass, and the action, which seemed to have been put on pause, started up again. Adam passed Freddy the menu, but she sat there, hardly able to take it in, the print dancing in front of her eyes. The thought of food was nauseating anyway. She ordered Dover sole, thinking she might be able to force some of it down and looking anywhere but at Joe, her thoughts racing.

What a fool she was! Nothing had changed, nothing! All her fine resolutions for keeping her head and her heart intact were trembling on the brink of ruin. Why, oh, why hadn't she realised how much she had missed him? How stupid not to understand why she felt so light-hearted today, so ridiculously indecisive over what to wear so that she could look her best for him! She had sworn that no man was going to have the power, ever again, to hurt her...

Adam asked, with quiet concern, if the sole was to her liking. She forced a smile, glancing briefly at him as she replied that it was delicious, and took a swallow of wine to force the next mouthful down. She sensed Joe was watching her closely and pushed aside the rising panic, calling on all her reserves. She laughed at something Adam said, and hated the searing jealousy that swept over her every time Nina and Joe smiled, spoke, laughed together. This wasn't what she wanted! It was so long since she had felt anything so acutely and had been so determined that her emotions should be inviolable that now they had been pierced she was stricken.

The half-eaten sole was whisked away and a crème caramel put in its place. This was easier to dispose of. She rather thought Adam Carlyon knew something was wrong, for he was being extremely kind, talking to her about things that demanded no response, so that by the time coffee came round she was feeling much calmer, and was able to talk back quite naturally.

'We're always struggling to find new ways of making money,' Adam was saying. 'The potential of a place such as ours is enormous and I like to think we use it to the full.'

Freddy nodded. She knew that apart from the main auditorium there was a small studio theatre tucked away under the eaves which put on the works of new writers and the more experimental plays that would not attract the larger audiences. There was foyer entertainment at lunch time, visiting ballet and opera companies as well as the Queen's own touring company.

An idea struck her and she said slowly, feeling her way, 'I wonder if you'd be interested in Atticus doing a programme about Queen's? You've built up such a tremendous reputation as being one of the best of the provincial theatres, it would be nice to let the ordinary public know about you.'

A flicker of interest showed in Adam's eyes. 'We did have an arts programme done on one of our guest directors last year, but it was more about him than Queen's.'

'It could be filmed over a number of weeks, taking in all aspects, perhaps following through one particular production...' Her voice, which had started off quietly ruminative, now gained speed and animation as the project began to take hold of her imagination, the adrenalin flowing as it always did at the beginning of any conception. She checked herself with a wry smile.

'No good getting too excited until we know if Atticus is interested. May I sound out Patrick Tyson and come back to you?' she asked.

When Adam replied, 'You may, and I look forward to hearing the outcome,' she felt a glow of satisfaction rise within her and she knew that she had regained her balance, was once more in full control of herself and what she had to do. She looked across the table at Joe for the first time since the meal had started, and the brown stare was directed her way, an enigmatic look on his face.

'I do hope we haven't been boring you with all our theatrical talk, Miss... I'm sorry, but I can't—how awful of me!—remember your name,' exclaimed Nina Welsh with beautiful embarrassment. 'Do forgive me.'

'Leigh,' offered Joe smoothly. 'Frederica Leigh, but I'm sure she'll be happy for you to call her Freddy,' and he waited for Freddy's 'Of course,' before he went on, 'It can hardly be boring for her, Nina. Frederica's used to it. She's one of us.'

'Really?' Nina turned her pansy eyes to Joe, and then on to Freddy. Freddy felt a flash of antagonism reach her from their depths.

She felt like saying—Don't worry, Nina, he's all yours.

'She works for Atticus,' Liz explained, and then hid a yawn, her eyes twinkling as she saw that Freddy had noticed.

Freddy suddenly knew what she had to do. She waited for a lull in the conversation and announced, 'I'm sorry, but I really have to go now.'

She rose to her feet and gave a smile that included the whole of the table, skimming over Joe. 'It's been a lovely evening and I enjoyed the play enormously. Unfortunately, I have a daughter who wakes regularly as clockwork and makes no concessions to Sunday being a day of rest.' She allowed herself a quick look at Joe and wished she hadn't.

Their departure was undertaken with incredible smoothness. Freddy managed to say quietly to Joe, 'If you don't want to leave now, I can easily take a taxi.' He didn't reply and there was something in his eyes that sent her panicking again, until she pulled herself together. If he was as furious as that look suggested it was tough luck! He'd soon get over it. Nina Welsh and a dozen others would help him.

The journey home was unremarkable other than for the silence between them. Freddy guessed that once they began to talk all hell would be let loose— and Joe angry was bad enough, but Joe angry at the wheel of a powerful car was dangerous! She was beginning, a little, to regret the disclosure of Megan in this way. She knew why she had done it, as a kind of flag-waving, to show that she was independent and not an appendage to Joe, or a threat to Nina or any other woman who considered she had a claim. But she could hardly admit that to Joe, for she would also have to admit to the feelings that had prompted the flag-waving.

Houdini greeted them with his usual enthusiasm. Freddy threw her coat over the banister and went into the sitting-room, saying, 'I'll put coffee on.'

Joe said abruptly, 'You needn't bother. I don't want any.'

'Well, I do,' retorted Freddy, and went into the kitchen to see to it. She didn't know whether she wanted any or not, but it was something to do. Her heart was beginning to pound and she stood still for a moment, marshalling thoughts and energy before re-entering the room. She found Joe studying Megan's photograph on the mantel, his face closed and an alarming grimness around his mouth.

'What is it you want to say, Joe?' she asked, her chin coming up as she stared steadily at him.

'I should think it's obvious, isn't it? Why didn't you tell me about her?'

'Does there have to be a reason?'

His mouth twisted. 'Oh, yes, I think so. It's not like you, Fred. Yes, there has to be a darned good reason.'

'Perhaps I thought someone else had told you. Liz, for instance...'

'If that had happened, I'd have said something.' Harsh impatience coloured his voice.

'Or maybe I considered you wouldn't be interested.'

'There were people you had never met before sitting around that table tonight, yet you thought they'd be interested.'

'I was telling them why I had to go.'

'And at the same time giving out information to me.' Joe's face darkened as if hit by the memory. 'Why like that? Suddenly? I can't understand your motives.'

'Women are incalculable,' she mocked. 'Haven't you realised that by now?' She sat down on the broad arm of the armchair and fondled Houdini who was uneasy, his black face looking from one to the other as they spoke, not liking the vibrations.

'I can't believe you're ashamed of her,' Joe said.

Freddy's head came up, eyes blazing as she lashed out, 'Certainly I'm not! What a foul thing to say! On the contrary, she's the best thing that's ever happened to me.'

'The best thing, and yet you don't talk about her?' Joe gave a wintry smile and she felt like slapping him.

'I do talk about her, of course I do,' she snapped, glowering. 'I just choose when to do so. Joe, what is all this? Why the fuss?'

'I feel as though you've hidden her from me, as if I were a threat to her.'

'Don't be ridiculous.' Yet there was enough in what he said for Freddy to be reminded again of his astuteness, of his ability to work tenaciously through a problem.

'I suppose you've had the brush-off in the past because of her,' he went on, his eyes boring into her relentlessly, 'but I bet you're not averse to using her as a deterrent when it suits you. Were you hoping I'd be put off, Frederica? Sorry to disappoint you; I like little girls, especially ones so appealing. How old is she?'

'Five. Her name is Megan. Now are you satisfied?'

'You have a sitter here tonight?'

Freddy stiffened, alerted by a subtle change in his voice.

'As a matter of fact, Megan's staying with friends.'

Lids dropped down over his eyes as he contemplated her for a moment. 'So it wasn't entirely true,' he remarked with silky softness, 'when you announced to all and sundry that you would be woken early. She's not here.'

'That's awfully discerning of you, Joe.' The sarcasm was rife in her voice.

'And we have the place to ourselves.' He gave one of his razor-edged smiles. The words dropped between them and hung full of implications.

'Oh!' Freddy allowed that shortest of exclamations to be full of surprise and enlightenment. She beamed a smile quite devoid of either humour or warmth. 'You think I've set up the ideal love-nest! Now you pat me on the shoulder and say, "There, there, little woman, I shall smooth away all your sexual frustrations, because you must have some, living here on your own without a man in sight,"' she rose, her voice hardening cynically, '"so let me warm you with my kisses and show you what a good lover I still am and how happy I can make you!" And then I swoon into your arms, for Sir Galahad has arrived riding not a white charger, but a red Tiger, and the princess is saved!'

Joe tut-tutted. 'You have a lousy script writer, Fred, and don't go putting words into my mouth that were never there. Women's Lib has altered all that humbug. Why should you have all the sexual frustrations? If you said that to me I'd be delighted.'

'I hope you're not trying to tell me that you have problems,' she said sarcastically, 'because I won't believe you.' She stared stonily at him. How dared he think she had contrived to have both Megan and Judith out of the house! As if their presence presented a problem in any case!

Joe walked slowly over to her, and although she felt like backing up Freddy stayed where she was, straight-backed, ready for battle. 'It can be very easy to drift into a situation,' he observed coolly, 'where there's a different head on the pillow every week, yet I can't see you falling into that trap, Frederica. No, you'd be choosy, and you'd make sure he knew all the conditions, the main one being to fit into your neat and tidy schedule... marked down in the ledger book under the appropriate entry. Well, I know the rules, and we know one another pretty well, I'd say, wouldn't you?' He paused and added significantly, 'But perhaps you have some scruples regarding David Herrick?'

Freddy said icily, 'Leave David out of this!'

'Willingly. The stage is set. We have the two principal players. Let's go to bed, Frederica.'

'You say the sweetest things, Joe. No.'

'I'm devastated. Is it something I did?'

'Poor Joe,' mocked Freddy. 'You can't understand why I'm not rushing into bed with you.'

'I know exactly why.' There was a taut silence between them, and his voice softened. 'You look so cool and poised. If this untouchable veneer is supposed to keep me at my distance, I'm afraid it's failing dismally.' He put up his hands and dexterously removed the combs and pins from her hair so that it fell in wonderful disarray to her shoulders. 'You've grown such a protective shell around you, Frederica, that if you don't watch out it'll smother you completely.'

'And you've given yourself the task of freeing me,' she ridiculed. 'You haven't changed, Joe. Still so arrogantly sure of yourself.'

'You've developed cold feet, Fred,' Joe told her softly, running his fingers through her hair. 'It's as simple as that.' He stroked her cheek and she flinched at his touch. 'You see?' he went on in a deep, gentle voice. 'You're frightened you might like it and forget to give me the brush-off. You have quite a good line in brush-offs, did you know, Fred? You have this way of raising your eyebrows fractionally and looking down your exquisite nose and your lips give a tiny, cold smile. It puts most men off. But for me it has the opposite effect.' His fingers traced the outline of her lips very lightly. 'Why don't you admit, Fred, that you have cold feet?'

'All right!' She slapped his hand away, eyes blazing, furious. 'Have it your own way.'

'That's better. We won't get anywhere wallowing around in self-deception.'

'We aren't going anywhere, Joe!'

Both hands came up this time and cupped her neck, thumbs gently following the line of her jaw in a mesmeric movement. 'You have more fire burning beneath that cool, keep-off façade than any woman I've ever met.' He gave a twisted smile. 'I speak from experience. You packed a pretty powerful punch eight years ago, Frederica.'

Steeling herself to ignore the magic of his touch, Freddy told him sardonically, 'So did you, Joe, so did you—and I'm sure you've improved since then, so perhaps it's just as well I got cold feet. Now neither of us will get burned.'

'That's what living is all about, Fred. It reminds you that you're still alive.'

'Be careful, Joe, you're beginning to sound like a character from a second-rate movie. You're an authority on living, then? Fancy yourself as the one to bring me alive, do you?' She gave an impatient exclamation and jerked her head away. 'Look, let's stop being frivolous...'

'I'm not feeling frivolous, Fred—bloody angry is what I'm feeling! What the hell are you doing to yourself? Bottling up all your emotions, frightened of becoming involved in case you might deviate from some preconceived plan, making out you're an icicle when I know damn well you're anything but!' He pulled her to him and began to kiss her, his hands either side of her head, holding her firm. Freddy struggled for a moment and then stood still, suffering the kisses with a blankness on her face, showing her contempt plainly. It was an onslaught of consummate skill as he touched her with his lips, seducing her with a gentleness behind which was a force, ready to be unleashed, and only held back by tremendous will-power. His mouth trailed across her flesh, leaving it on fire, kissing her neck, her cheeks, her eyelids, while his hands moved to her shoulders and then journeyed down her body, holding her against him so that the feel and shape of him impressed upon her mind, her senses relearning his smell, his texture, his strength. Her softness complemented his hardness, her roundness his leanness, and those hands, those marvellous hands touched and caressed, and sneaked their way past the silken folds of fabric and cupped her breast. The fire within her leaped to his touch as his fingers teased and smoothed and his lips teased and charmed.

Enough! This was madness. Freddy turned her face away and brought up a hand to stay his. So far she had not responded, but she could not hold out much longer, and she had some pride left. Her heart seemed to be pounding through the whole of her body, and under the impeccable grey suit jacket where her hands had treacherously found themselves—but were now severely on the outside—she had felt the thumping of his heart, and the warmth of his armpits, and the tapering bony ridges of his ribs.

With precise delicacy, Joe put her from him.

'An icicle,' he drawled silkily, 'is what you are not.' He stretched out a hand and with mocking arrogance drew the folds of her dress back into place, and the irony stretched like a taut rope between them.

Freddy felt as though she was running a fever and yet still felt cold. How easy it would be to give in . . .

'My script might be a lousy one,' she said scornfully, 'but you seem to be able to follow it pretty well.' She was under control now, although her breast still had the imprint of his hand upon it. 'But we're playing an out-of-date scenario. We've been through it all before and we're different people now.' She gave a funny little shrug of the shoulders and her lips curved downwards derisively. 'I'm not going to be such a fool as to deny that there is this physical attraction between us, but I suspect you could become rather like a drug, Joe. And for me to become an addict would be even more foolish.' She held his stare, chin up, and added with finality, 'Goodnight.'

Joe stood for a moment, eyelids drooping, lips a thin line, and then he strolled to the door, half turned and drawled, 'Goodnight, princess. Sleep well.' And, giving a mocking smile, he left.

Freddy heard the front door slam, and in the kitchen the noise of the percolator mingled tunefully with Houdini's snores.

# CHAPTER FOUR

JACK FROST arrived with December, laying icy fingers everywhere. Days fell into their familiar pattern, the familiarity soothing. Mrs Mallory slipped on the ice and bruised a knee, but was back the next day, as indomitable as ever. As term neared its end Judith's spirits rose. She was spending the Christmas holiday with her fiancé in America; the flight was booked and her suitcase was at the ready.

Megan was invited to play with Michael Carlyon and his sister, Victoria, nicknamed Plum, a gorgeous eighteen-month-old girl who followed them around like an adoring puppy. And Liz and Freddy continued their exploration into friendship with increasing satisfaction.

Patrick Tyson showed interest in the Queen's Theatre project and began talks with Adam Carlyon. For Freddy, unusually busy, the end of term came as rather a surprise. This was traditionally highlighted by a carol service, a nativity play and a party for the schoolchildren. At the nativity play, Liz and Freddy sat together among the other parents, and fought back a tear as Michael and Megan, dressed as a shepherd and an angel, appeared onstage. They glanced at each other and smiled sheepishly. The day after term ended Judith flew to the States and Freddy's parents arrived to take Megan back with them for the Christmas holiday. Freddy was aiming to join them later in the week.

Megan was waiting by the window long before her grandparents were due, dressed in a bright red jumper, a tartan skirt and red tights. She had just finished writing a note to Father Christmas, with help from her mother, to make sure he knew they would be at Boston. It would be a terrible thing if he made the mistake of delivering her presents here!

When the dark blue Ford estate turned the corner, she leaped to her feet, crying, 'They're here, Mummy! Granny and Grandad are here!'

Freddy watched her daughter fly down the path to fling her arms round Mr and Mrs Leigh as they emerged from the car. She waited for the threesome to come in, and kissed and hugged her parents, satisfied that they looked no different from their last visit.

The same feeling could not justifiably be found in Catherine Leigh as she studied her daughter. She hated to fuss, but found the words coming out unbidden. 'Darling, you look as though you need this holiday!'

Freddy said brightly, 'I'm fine, Mum, honestly.' She met her mother's dubious eye and added firmly, 'You know I never have much colour, and I'm really as tough as old boots!' With that Catherine had to be satisfied.

Edmund Leigh was standing at the window watching birds pecking at crumbs on the bird-table. Tall and thin, he was a semi-retired solicitor with a keen interest in wildlife. His brown hair was remarkably free from grey, and it was from him that Freddy had inherited her height.

Catherine Leigh had drawn Megan on to her lap and was listening to the story of the letter to Father Christmas while Freddy wandered over to the window and tucked her arm through her father's. They watched the antics of a robin as he pecked at the nuts, chased off by an impudent sparrow.

'Cheeky devils, sparrows,' observed Edmund, and patting his daughter's arm added, 'Lunch, now, I think.'

Freddy insisted on taking them to a local restaurant, saying it wasn't often she was able to treat them to a meal, and because of the weather forecast which promised snow, Edmund decided to start back home immediately after.

He stood on the steps of Dean Close while his wife settled Megan and 'that darned dog', as he called Houdini, into the car. He eyed his daughter thoughtfully. 'Your mother's a little worried about you, my dear,' he confided mildly. 'Been overdoing things a bit?'

Freddy squeezed his arm. 'Dad, there's nothing wrong with me that a whiff of east wind can't blow away,' she said, and grinned, for the wind that came off the North Sea straight from Siberia was notoriously bracing in the summer and bitterly cold in the winter.

'Hum, well, take care of yourself, and drive carefully. Where are you off to tomorrow?'

'Yorkshire. We're doing winter location work for *Wuthering Heights*.'

'They've had large falls of snow up there, so mind what you're doing.' Edmund bent to kiss her.

Freddy followed him down the path, commanding, 'Mind how *you* go!'

She gave Megan a kiss through the window, saying with mock severity, 'Be good, brat,' and Catherine said, 'She's always good, aren't you, darling?'

Freddy waved the car out of sight and walked back into the house, feeling a little bereft.

That evening she went to a concert with David Herrick, her work colleague. It was a programme she favoured, but for once she couldn't lose herself in the music. The reason she knew well enough. She had spied Joe sitting a few rows in front and he was not alone. Concentration from then on was hopeless, and she tensed up with irritation. If you're going to be like this every time you see Joe Corey with another woman, then you're in for a hard time, she told herself furiously, and made a huge effort to blank him out. Coming slowly down the stairs as the audience filed out of the concert hall it seemed inevitable that Joe and his companion should be coming down the opposite staircase at the same time. Their eyes held for a moment, Freddy's cool, Joe's veiled, and then he gave her a small, secret smile before turning to talk to his partner. Soon he was lost in the crowd.

David was in fine form, making her laugh, showing an interest in the *Wuthering Heights* programme. They went for a meal and she almost forgot Joe. She cried off from prolonging the evening, giving the early start of the journey the following day as the excuse, and closing the door on David with relief. As she lay, unable to sleep, she knew her life was changed. Joe Corey had laid his hands on her and made her body come alive and sing to his special tune. Of course, in time she would forget, but seeing him tonight had awakened a welter of feelings that could not be ignored.

With family presents secure in the boot, Freddy pointed the Renault northwards to the M1. It was sunny, but cold. She took her time, taking stops for exercise and refreshment, bypassed Bradford and headed for Skipton. On the other side of Kettlewell she pulled into the car park of the King's Head hotel. She could see no signs of the Atticus vans, or any other vehicle that she could recognise as being part of the team, and guessed she was the first to arrive.

The hotel had breathtaking views of Great Whernside to the east and Langstrothdale to the west, and was warm and friendly. She unpacked the few items of clothing she would be needing— thick cords, warm underwear, sweaters, woollen socks—finally hanging a fur-lined parka into the wardrobe, and placing sheepskin boots underneath. The sound of vehicles outside made her look through the window to see the caravans being pulled by Land Rovers trailing their way into the car park, followed by a number of cars and Transits. 'It seems I have a crew,' she murmured, and wondered if her producer, Tiny Dakin, had arrived yet. She was a little surprised not to have been met by him, as she thought he had been planning to arrive the day before so that he could check everything would go smoothly the following day.

She washed and changed, and went in search of the dining-room. The first person she saw on entering was Joe.

He was sitting at a table for two, a half-filled wine-glass and an opened bottle set before him. When he saw Freddy appear in the doorway, he rose to his feet and watched her walk towards him. His face was carefully enigmatic. Apart from the slight heightening of colour, Freddy could easily have been keeping a longstanding engagement. Her cool gaze flickered round the room, acknowledging some of the crew already seated with a quick smile. She was wearing a knitted jacket the colour of crushed raspberries over a long-sleeved shirt checked in the same two-toned colour. A grey wool skirt, smooth over the hips, flaring generously to the hem, allowed her stride to be uninhibited, meeting mid-calf, dark grey suede boots. She was a good mover, with an unconscious fluidity that attracted the eye. There was a friendly smile on her lips for the benefit of onlookers, but her eyes showed plainly what her feelings were.

Joe moved leisurely round the table, pulling out the other chair for her to be seated. Freddy did so, waiting until he regained his place before demanding, 'And to what do I owe this unexpected honour, Joseph?'

He reached for the bottle of wine and filled her glass. 'To a cockerel,' he offered.

Freddy took a sip of wine. It was a Hock, cool and delicious. Her heartbeat had settled down to its usual rhythm and she was in control again. Why ever had she supposed, she wondered resignedly, that it would be easy to keep out of his way?

'A cockerel?' She considered his grave nod of assent, not hurrying into speech. She studied the wine in her glass, aware of him sitting opposite, the epitome of unconcerned ease, wearing a jacket in subtle shades of browns, a nice tweedy tie, light tan shoes with dashing pale lemon socks. His expression was similar to the one of the previous evening, when their glances had met across the stairway of the concert hall—the same secret smile curving his lips. She marvelled at how steady her hand was as it held the wine glass, knowing her body had shifted into a higher gear because of him.

Freddy lifted her eyes and, taking a careful breath, set the glass down before saying, 'My producer, Tiny Dakin, is plucking, training, chasing, or eating—a cockerel?' She tossed off these offerings with due seriousness, adding curiously, 'What colour was it?' even while she was thinking, Tiny Dakin isn't here and Joe Corey is. Three or four days of Joe...

Joe's mouth tugged at the corners, but he controlled the smile from breaking out. 'I doubt Tiny cares a damn what colour it was. Rumour has it that he's been plagued by a rogue cockerel for the past week, and driven to desperation—it was waking him from a perch in his pear tree at some ungodly hour in the morning—he decided to bag it unawares as dusk fell. Unfortunately for Tiny, as dusk fell so did he! The ground broke his fall and his leg.' He watched with approval as Freddy burst out laughing.

'Oh, dear! Poor Tiny—we shouldn't laugh.' She sobered and came down to hard facts. 'So Patrick has sent you in his place?'

Joe smirked with due humility. 'I seemed to be the only person available at such short notice.'

'I expect,' Freddy announced with kindly patronage, 'you'll manage.' She picked up the menu, enjoying his bark of laughter.

Half-way through the meal, which could hardly have been described as intimate, surrounded as they eventually were by crew members and actors, conversation going from table to table, Joe asked, 'Did you enjoy the concert last night?'

'Yes, thank you,' Freddy replied. 'Did you?'

'It was my sister's choice, but yes, I enjoyed it.'

'Your sister?'

'She was staying with me for a few days.' One brow rose quizzically as Joe went on, 'I would have introduced you to her, but you disappeared rather too quickly.'

Coffee was served in the lounge, where a large open fire was burning, and everyone gathered to note details for the next day. Freddy said goodnight early and stood for a while looking out of her bedroom window. The fells were covered in snow and looked eerie and remote, just right for Heathcliff and Cathy and *Wuthering Heights*. Her thoughts turned to Joe. So he had taken his sister to the concert! But that didn't change anything really.

During the next few days temperatures remained below freezing and made shooting hazardous and uncomfortable. It was easy to get lost on the moors, so the team proceeded in convoy to avoid missing the locations and each other. They would be returning in the spring to take more shots, but spring seemed a long way away as they tramped through snow drifts and drank endless cups of coffee and soup to keep warm.

Joe was a director's dream. He was there when Freddy wanted him, sorting out problems quickly and calmly as they arose, yet not breathing down her neck, and he was ready to chew over a shot and give advice if asked. The filming was absorbing and hard, and when failing light cut down the working day they would all go back to the King's Head, check through the next day's schedule, eat dinner and gather together afterwards in the lounge. These evenings were rich in conversation and full of stories and philosophising, Freddy adding her penn'orth and joining in the arguments with gusto. There were the usual flirtations going on. Most would fizzle out, some might not. The actress playing the role of Cathy was greatly enamoured of Joe, although to give him his due he gave her no encouragement.

On the third evening, someone banged on Freddy's door and shouted that she was wanted in Joe's room. When she tapped on the door and he called to come in she found he was on the telephone. He put a hand over the mouthpiece and said, 'Tyson. He wants a word with you,' and then went on with his conversation. Soon after, he passed the phone to Freddy, who spoke to Patrick, bringing him up to date.

While she was talking, Joe sat reading an evening paper. Patrick made some amusing comment regarding Tiny Dakin, making her laugh, and she said, 'I'm sorry about Tiny, of course. Give him my love, but his substitute is more than competent and makes up for Tiny's absence.' She listened a moment, nodded, gave a soft laugh, and said goodbye. She put the phone down and looked across the room to Joe, who was deeply engrossed in the newsprint. 'In case you weren't listening,' Freddy said, 'I want to repeat my thanks for your help, Joe. You've been invaluable. I've always wanted to do *Wuthering Heights*, and naturally I want it to be good. This part of it will be, thanks to you.'

Joe lifted his eyes above the paper, replied a laconic, 'Thanks,' and then added bluntly, 'I don't think you should be too enthusiastic in singing my praises to Patrick Tyson.'

Freddy stared. What the hell was the matter with the man now?

'Just what is that supposed to mean?' she demanded, and Joe shrugged, tossing down the paper—it was a good thing he did or else Freddy might have snatched it from him—and linked his hands behind his head.

'He might become jealous,' he said, looking for all the world as though he had made some comment as trivial as the weather.

'Why jealous?' Tight-lipped, the words came out with clipped enunciation.

'I know you tend to go around in blinkers, but you must know that he, for want of a more graphic term, fancies you? Women usually do know, and although you can be naïve, I've never thought you unintelligent.'

'How wonderful for me!' Fury made her nearly speechless. 'And I suppose I've been kept on at Atticus because I've got the boss hooked, is that it? The one thing I could cling on to with any kind of dignity was my work and you have just smashed that to smithereens, damn you! All I've achieved in the past three years you've just reduced to a nasty taste in the mouth!'

'You're over-reacting,' Joe told her in a bored voice. 'And that's ridiculous and you know it. Tyson's too good a businessman to allow his feelings to over-ride his professional judgement.'

The calmness of his voice incensed her. 'Perhaps you think I'm his mistress already?'

'I don't think you are, yet.'

'I suppose I should be thankful for small mercies.'

'He's an attractive man, with power. A heady combination, and his marriage isn't everything it should be. You wouldn't be the first, of course, but I understand Dinah usually turns a blind eye. I doubt she would if you became Tyson's latest. It would be too close for comfort. Beware of Dinah, Frederica, she's a lethal lady.' He picked up the paper and began to read, adding with silky softness, 'I notice you haven't denied my remarks about Tyson and you.'

Freddy struggled with the idea of doing him physical violence. How could she be thanking him for his help one minute and then wanting to murder him the next? Impossible man! She unclenched her fists and made a great effort, but her voice showed her feelings plainly. 'I suppose you have good intentions,' she said, 'but they are misplaced. I can take care of myself, thank you very much!' and she took great pleasure in slamming the door.

When she gained her room she threw herself on the bed and stared darkly up at the ceiling. Part of the trouble was that he was right, damn him! She had known for some time that Patrick, given the least bit of encouragement, would enjoy more than a boss-employee relationship, but she had never given him any encouragement, and thought Joe infuriatingly perceptive for noticing.

She brought a cool, professional manner down to breakfast, and only spoke when spoken to where Joe was concerned. It didn't seem to bother him. There was an air of controlled haste as they set off for the final day's shoot. More snow had been forecast and it was a race against time.

Freddy stamped her feet and held her hands under her armpits for warmth. The caravans, two used as changing-rooms, the third as canteen, afforded some degree of shelter, but the sky was getting greyer and lower all the time and they had to finish that day, come what may.

When the last scene was taken everyone sent up a cheer and packing away began. When everything was loaded engines started and were warmed up, ready to drive back to the hotel from where the production team and the actors would go their separate ways. Freddy was staying on a further night as she had no wish to tackle the journey to Boston so late in the day.

She now stood by the side of the Renault, waiting to see that everyone had transport back to the King's Head. She was tired, but had a positive feeling in her bones that they had some excellent film in the can. She watched Joe walk across to one of the Transits and thought about his comments on Patrick Tyson the night before. Really, the man was too dictatorial for words! Didn't he credit her with any sense?

Whatever the hiccup was over by the Transit it seemed to be resolved, for the van drove off slowly. Joe walked towards her on snow that had been packed down by feet and wheels, the collar of his sheepskin upturned.

'I'm told you're not returning with the mob,' he began abruptly, 'that you're going into Skipton on your own, is that right?'

Freddy stiffened at his tone, and her 'Yes' came out a touch defensive.

'Then I'll come with you.'

She raised her brows in wonderful surprise. 'You want to go to Skipton?' she asked.

'No, dammit, I do not, but it's a crazy idea for you to go off on your own. Individual cars were told to stay with the vans ...'

'But that was so that no one would miss the locations,' answered Freddy patiently. The volume of noise increased as one by one the vehicles passed by. When the last of the caravans had disappeared

over the brow of the hill, she observed sardonically, 'Well, it looks like I'm stuck with you.'

'It's the other way round—I'm stuck with you!'
Joe's face darkened with exasperated anger. 'Con-
found it, woman, have you looked at that sky? I
have absolutely no wish to be scouring the countryside searching every snowdrift in a blizzard which
anyone with any modicum of sense could tell is on
the way!'

Freddy eyed him thoughtfully, turned to con-
sider the sky and then the barren landscape and
held up her hands peacefully. 'Sorry. You're right.
It wasn't a good idea. I'll be grateful of your
company.' She held out the keys. 'Would you care
to drive?'

The grim lines on Joe's face softened and an
eyebrow shot up. 'I didn't think I'd ever get an
apology out of you, Fred.'

'I was always brought up to believe that an
apology showed strength, not weakness—but if you
rub my nose in it, you might never get another.'
She opened the door and settled herself in, pushing
back the hood of the parka and shaking her hair
free.

Joe slid behind the wheel, his eyes scanning the
sky anxiously. The engine took a few goes to catch
and as they finally drove off in the opposite
direction from the team the first flakes began to
fall.

Seeing them, Freddy said pleasantly, 'If you say
I told you so...' and left the rest of the sentence
to Joe's imagination.

He gave an absent smile and asked, 'Am I allowed to ask why you want to go into Skipton?'

'There's a book I want to get for my father for Christmas. A book on birds, just released. I thought if I got it today I wouldn't have to delay my journey tomorrow.' She consulted the map she had been studying and added, 'We turn off here.'

They travelled for a few miles and then Joe pulled up, the wipers barely coping with the snowfall. He looked at the map and frowned. 'I think it would have been better to have made for the main road instead of trying to cut through.' He peered through the windscreen at the snow, which showed no signs of letting up, and at the light, which was fading rapidly. 'Do we go back and make for the A65 or carry on and hope for the best?'

'Are you asking me, or just thinking out loud? If we turn back we have further to go... and the road looks OK.'

'Hmm...' Joe frowned, thinking hard, and then said, 'Ahead it is.'

Some minutes later the outline of three cottages came into view and Freddy murmured, 'A bit isolated up here, isn't it?' as they approached. The car skidded on a rut and she glanced anxiously at Joe, but his expression showed reassuring concentration. Then he muttered, 'Hello, what's this?' and she followed the direction of his eyes and saw what had caught his attention. A figure of a man was running out of the middle cottage, down the path and through the gate, his arms waving wildly to attract their attention.

'I'd say he wants us to stop, wouldn't you?' drawled Joe, applying his foot to the brakes gingerly, gently slowing the Renault so that they were barely moving by the time they drew level. Joe wound down the window and a blast of cold air and snow swept into the car. The stranger flung himself on to the door, as if to detain them by force if necessary.

'Thank God you've come along!' he gasped, fighting for breath. 'I'm sorry, but I need help, my wife's started in labour, she's three weeks early and I don't know what to do. It's our first and...'

'Take your time,' Joe said calmly. 'If we can help, we will.' He glanced at the inadequate clothing of the young man—he was in a sweater and trousers which were rapidly becoming white with snow—and added, 'Suppose you go back into the house and we'll join you there.'

The young man hesitated, as if by releasing his hold on the car they would disappear over the horizon, and Freddy smiled reassuringly, urging, 'We'll come, I promise.'

He nodded and ran back along the road, down the path, disappearing through the open front door.

Joe turned to look at her and drawled, 'This is beginning to feel like a lousy B-movie,' and as they got out of the car he added drily, 'Let's hope he's just panicking.'

Struggling through the snow up to the house, Freddy fervently hoped so too.

# CHAPTER FIVE

THE young man introduced himself as Colin Baxter, and he gazed at them anxiously as they walked in. When Freddy asked, 'Are you sure you're not worrying unnecessarily?' he shook his head and replied, 'I don't think so, but come in and see what you think.'

He pushed open the inner door and they followed him, hearing him say comfortingly, 'Marion, you won't be on your own now, love.' He glanced back, adding, 'I'm sorry, I don't know your names...'

'Hello, Marion,' Freddy said, giving what she hoped was a confident smile, as she moved towards the young woman, heavily pregnant, who was lying on a couch made up into a bed. 'I'm Freddy, and this is Joe. How are you feeling?'

'Like I'm on an express train without any stops,' Marion said breathlessly, giving a plucky smile.

Freddy nodded sympathetically. 'You want to say—"Hey, can we take a break now, I'm not sure I'm ready!"' Marion groaned a laugh, for that was exactly right.

'You have no phone,' Joe stated, his eyes assessing the cottage. 'And there's no help to be had from the people either side?'

Colin shook his head, shrugging on his coat. 'One's a holiday place, and the other's owned by an elderly couple who have gone to their daughter's for Christmas. I was going to take Marion to her mother's tomorrow...' His voice trailed remorsefully.

'You couldn't have anticipated this would happen,' soothed Freddy, taking off her parka and throwing it across a chair. 'First babies are unpredictable.'

'I shall go for the midwife——' Colin began.

Joe broke in, 'Can't I go for you? Although I'm afraid I'm not familiar with the district.'

Colin considered this and shook his head. 'I'd better go, you might get lost, but if you'll stay with Marion I shall feel a lot happier.'

'Of course we'll stay,' assured Freddy, smiling, and wiping Marion's face with a flannel she found in a bowl on the table.

'You'd better go now,' Joe said, 'before it gets totally dark. Is it far?'

'The next village but one.' Colin took Marion's hand and bent to kiss her. 'Marion, darling, I'll be back as soon as I can.' Then he hurried from the room, Joe following him.

'How often are the contractions?' Freddy asked.

Marion murmured, 'Every four minutes.'

Freddy's heart sank, but she asked calmly, 'What do you know about having babies?'

'I thought I knew quite a lot, but now I'm not so sure.' Marion blew out a breath. 'It's awful to say it, but I'm glad Colin's gone. He's so worried, poor darling, he's better out of the way.' A contraction began and she rode it out, and when it was finished, sank back on the pillows, gasping, 'I don't think help is going to arrive in time, do you?'

'I'm afraid I don't think so either, so we'll have to manage by ourselves, won't we?' Freddy replied cheerfully.

'Do you know anything about having babies?' Marion asked.

'Well, I've had one, although she's five now,' admitted Freddy, 'but it's a bit different being on the receiving end rather than the producing one.' She checked her watch as Marion began another contraction and observed calmly, 'That was pretty strong, wasn't it?' Marion nodded and closed her eyes wearily. Freddy went in search of the kitchen and filled a kettle as Joe arrived in the doorway. She glanced at him and remarked quietly, 'I don't believe this, Joe, I just don't believe this is happening to us! Will you pinch me so I can wake up?'

'We're sharing the same nightmare,' Joe answered drily. 'Is she going to have the child now?'

'She's certainly going to have the child now, and the nearest I've been to something like this is watching *Gone With The Wind*. I have, suddenly, the greatest sympathy with Scarlett O'Hara!' She indicated the kettle. 'Hot water always seems to be top priority in such cases and I hope I'll get full marks from the midwife. How long will Colin be?'

'He wasn't saying much, and what came out wasn't particularly sensible. He was in a pretty bad state.'

'Most husbands are with their first.' Freddy washed her hands at the sink and stood, dripping, looking for a towel.

'Was yours?'

Above their heads was an indoor clothes line. She pulled down a clean towel and dried herself. 'He was dining an important client at the time,' she said matter-of-factly, and walked through into the living-room without looking at him. 'Marion, can we find clean sheets or towels?' she asked. 'Anything will do.'

'In the airing cupboard, bathroom,' instructed Marion. 'Baby's things are in the case in the bedroom.' She grimaced and bit her bottom lip, perspiration standing out on her forehead. 'I'm so sorry... I know how awful this must be for you both.' She waited and blew out a breath, squinting at her watch. 'It's every two minutes now.'

'Get cracking, Joe,' ordered Freddy calmly, keeping her expression free of anxiety. So much could go wrong, but now wasn't the time to be thinking negatively. 'Women are having babies every minute of the day. It's called natural reproduction.'

Marion gave a sob of a laugh and held out her hand. 'How nice you are,' she said.

Freddy took the hand and held it in a strong grip. 'Thank you. So is Joe. Do you want him to be here, or not? He's no Doctor Kildare, but he holds hands really well.'

'Among other things,' added Joe whimsically, appearing at her elbow. He gave Marion one of his devastating smiles. 'How about me understudying Colin?'

'You can't possibly want to,' protested Marion, and then, 'here comes another... please stay, Joe.'

'Then I shall,' he promised, dragging up a stool and taking her hands in his. He waited until the contraction passed and asked, 'What brings you and Colin to live here? Do you like it?' He glanced at the shelves of books in the corner. 'Psychology, secondary education—is Colin a teacher?'

'We both are, at a school near Ilkley. Not me now, of course... And yes, we like it here.' Her voice sharpened and she said, 'I want to push!'

Freddy replied cheerfully, 'Then push. Who are we to argue with Mother Nature?'

So far as Freddy could tell, Marion's labour seemed to be following a normal pattern. The next few minutes were fraught, with Marion working hard, encouraged by Freddy and Joe, and when the baby at last arrived into the outside world, Freddy cried triumphantly, 'Marion, you marvellous girl, you've done it!'

Marion asked tiredly, 'Is it all right?' and Joe said, 'Shouldn't it cry?' Then there was a splutter and a strangled croak, and finally a gloriously indignant yell!

Freddy and Joe laughed out loud and Freddy, her hands full of warm, wet baby, cried, 'You have a daughter, Marion, and she's beautiful.' Freddy felt the adjective allowable. This funny bundle of humanity, red and wrinkled and squashed and far from clean, was incredibly beautiful, despite everything. Tears were rolling down Marion's cheeks and she was too full up to speak. Joe handed Freddy a sheet and she wrapped the baby carefully in it, first wiping the still screaming indignant face, and then put her into her mother's arms. The screaming stopped miraculously as Marion cooed love words and kissed her.

Freddy covered Marion with a blanket and murmured to Joe, 'I'm leaving the cord. I read somewhere it's best not to do anything.' She straightened and pushed the hair from her face. 'Thank God that's over!' She heaved a sigh and grinned weakly at Joe who said quietly, 'Well done, Fred. You excelled yourself.'

Freddy replied simply, 'So did you,' and they exchanged a shared-experience smile across the couch.

'I can't thank you both enough,' said Marion emotionally, gazing adoringly down at her daughter. 'What would I have done without you?' She turned her eyes to Freddy. 'Do you mind if I call the baby after your husband? I've always liked the name Josephine.'

'I told you he could hold hands good, didn't I?' quipped Freddy. 'And Joe will be thrilled, won't you, Joe?' She refused to catch his eye and bent to touch the baby's soft cheek with the back of a finger, smiling as she murmured gently, 'Hello, Josephine,' adding as though an afterthought, 'But he's not my husband, Marion,' primly, 'we're just good friends.'

Marion laughed, as she was expected to, and exclaimed, 'Oh, dear, I thought...' and Joe let her off the hook and said, 'She sounds just like a wife, I agree. Do this, do that. A typical bossy Aries female. She'd have me if she could, of course.'

'Of course,' agreed Marion, smiling.

'... but I'm too clever for her!' Joe assumed a revoltingly smug expression. Before Freddy could suitably reply there came a hard rapping on the front door which Joe went to answer.

Freddy crossed to the window, pulled back the curtain and peered out into the darkness. Snow was still falling. 'The cavalry's arrived, Marion,' she announced, a tremendous feeling of relief sweeping over her. 'A Land Rover-type ambulance. Colin's here too.'

From then on everything was out of their hands. The ambulance men took over, and when Marion was comfortable she was carried out, wrapped up in blankets, the baby cocooned inside. She called out her thanks again, echoed by Colin, who was barely conscious of their existence and had eyes only for his wife and daughter. Finally the ambulance drove off and the front door was shut. Everywhere seemed abnormally quiet.

Freddy looked round the room as if she had never seen it before. She said flatly, 'That's that, then,' and gave a laugh. 'So much for getting Dad's book at Skipton.' She glanced at Joe. 'I didn't see the Renault outside.'

'No, I've put it round the back in a kind of lean-to. We're not attempting to drive back in this tonight. You needn't scowl like that,' he ordered firmly. 'If you use your head you'll see I'm talking sense.'

'I'm not scowling, I'm thinking.'

'It looks painful. I've asked Colin to ring the hotel and let them know we're all right and what's happened.' Joe stared at her, eyes narrowed. 'What's the matter? Is the idea of being holed up

here with me too obnoxious? Don't worry, you're
quite safe.'

'Oh, don't be ridiculous!' flared Freddy and
turned away, beginning to strip the sheets from the
couch with more force than was necessary, her body
taut as she fought for control.

Two hands grasped her shoulders and forced her
round, and Joe pulled her on to his chest, his voice
calm as he suggested, 'Why don't you have a good
bawl and get it over with?'

She allowed herself to let go and be comforted
and when the bout of crying was over accepted the
offer of his handkerchief, blew her nose and said,
'I'm sorry. I've done.'

'Be my guest. Can I have my turn now? A gently
nurtured sensitive type like myself, why, the whole
thing's sent me all of a tremble!'

Freddy laughed weakly. She felt utterly drained
and was glad to lean against Joe's chest for a
moment. How marvellous he was! She could never
have coped without him; he had given her such
confidence, and how wonderful he had been with
Marion, so gentle and sweet. Her cheek rested
against the wool of his sweater and one of Joe's
hands was pressed lightly, palm outspread, on her
back, the other cupped her neck and that particular area of flesh was coming awake, as if
drawing life from the contact. The tempo of her
body changed and her senses sharpened.

Perhaps she gave an involuntary movement, a
tensing up, for Joe put her unhurriedly away from
him, saying, 'I wonder if the worthy Colin has any

liquor on the premises? He told us to make ourselves at home, so we'll take him at his word.'

'I think I'm hungry,' announced Freddy in some surprise. 'I'll clear up here and then raid the larder.' Upstairs she found there was a tiny bathroom and two bedrooms, the smaller one made ready for the new baby, the main one with a double bed. All the ceilings and floors sloped and the temperature was quite low, despite the portable stove at the top of the stairs.

In the larder she found home-made bread, cheese, eggs and milk and there was a coffee grinder and beans. Joe made up the fire with logs he found in a store outside, and unearthed a bottle of red wine from a cupboard. They ate hungrily from plates on their knees in front of the fire.

Replete, Freddy groaned a sigh. 'My bones ache,' she announced in surprise. 'Why should they ache? I didn't have the baby!' She lay back in the chair and looked round the room. 'No television,' she observed, 'but a radio... they're really opting for the simple life, aren't they? No good expecting to be recognised for our artistic talents—except, I do see a copy of *Wandering Man* up there on the shelf, Joe. Isn't that nice?' She fell silent, thinking about Colin and Marion and their baby, her thoughts going to her own family. She asked pensively, 'Are your parents still alive, Joe?'

'No. They died a few years back.' He was lying in the other armchair, relaxed, a glass of wine in one hand, eyes closed.

'Do your sisters still live in Devon?'

'One does, she married a farmer. The other lives in Belgium.'

'Are you close?'

'Yes. I take my role of favourite uncle very seriously. I like their husbands. I visit when I can.' He took a drink of wine, eyes half-hooded as he looked across at her. 'And yours?'

'Both still alive,' she replied thoughtfully. 'I can't imagine a time when they won't be there, but I know it will have to come. They're wonderful with Megan. She adores them.'

Joe leaned across and refilled her glass. He regarded her for a moment, put down the bottle and leaned back again. 'What went wrong with your marriage, Frederica?'

She didn't answer for a long moment, staring into the fire. 'We were neither of us what the other hoped for,' she said at last. 'As simple as that. I look back on that period of my life with amazement and dismay. We were a great disappointment to each other.' She sipped the wine. Her body felt heavy; it seemed a great effort to lift the glass to her lips. There was a small table lamp lit in the corner, casting a subdued area of light, the rest came from the flickering flames of the fire. 'Do you think we shall be able to leave tomorrow? Silly question. I want to ask what we shall do if we can't, but that's just as silly.' Her eyes wandered the room, taking in the crocheted covers, the patchwork cushions, the home-made rugs on the floor. The cottage was very appealing. A corn dolly hanging from the chimney breast made her think of Megan and she said ruefully, 'I have to get to Boston for Christmas

Eve even if it means taking to skis, pulling a sledge myself! Imagine all the awkward questions from Megan if her presents aren't there Christmas morning! She still believes in the good St Nicholas, Santa Claus, whoever.' A yawn escaped her before she could control it.

Joe had taken a book from the shelf and was turning the pages. He said, without looking up, 'I should get off to bed.'

Freddy stayed where she was. The clock seemed to be ticking with unnatural loudness. She watched Joe who was now deeply into the book and finally rose to her feet, saying, 'Goodnight, then, Joe,' and received a glance and a relaxed, 'Goodnight, Fred,' in return.

The bedroom was not inviting. It was too cold to strip off completely, so she went as far as long-sleeved thermal T-shirt and pants, keeping on the warm woollen socks, and wrapped herself in the eiderdown and waited for sleep. Which didn't come. She heard Joe come upstairs, tensing, relaxing as his footsteps made their way into the bathroom and subsequently down the stairs once more.

Although she felt physically tired, her brain was having a field-day. It seemed hours later and she still hadn't slept. She peered at her watch face and found she had forgotten to wind it, then lay for a few minutes analysing her sleeplessness. She sat up, pulling the eiderdown round her shoulders before padding quietly down the stairs.

Opening the door into the living-room, Freddy saw Joe standing by the window, one curtain pulled back. He made a movement as if to turn and then stopped. She crossed, trailing the eiderdown, to peer at the clock on the mantel, groaning, 'Two o'clock! Is that all?' and soft-footed over and stood by his shoulder. 'What's the weather doing?' she asked, and stared through the glass, her eyes adjusting to the dark.

'Still snowing, but not so thickly,' Joe answered quietly.

Freddy studied his back. It was not conducive to conversation. 'How about us changing places for the rest of the night?' she suggested. 'I don't suppose you've slept much, have you?'

'I'm fine.'

The tone was dismissive. 'Ah, come on, Joe, I want you to. It'll make me feel better.' She walked back to the couch, threw down the eiderdown and sat, possession being nine-tenths of the law. 'You need your sleep. Stop being stubborn.'

'Frederica,' warned Joe pleasantly, his back still to her, 'if you don't get your butt off that couch in one minute...'

Freddy felt delicious tinglings sneaking their way through her body, wonderful remembered sensations of living dangerously. She said with reasonable curiosity, 'If I don't, what shall you do?'

The words dropped provocatively into the silence, and after a moment Joe let go of the curtain and slowly turned to contemplate her thoughtfully. His face was only partly lit by the flames from the fire and it was difficult to read his expression, while Freddy, on the other hand, was illuminated quite well. She made her own expression one of interested questioning. When he made no reply, she went on, allowing an amused mocking note to creep into her voice, 'I'm not a fragile little woman who needs cosseting, you know. I must say you've learned some manners since the old days—you'd have taken me up on the offer eight years ago.'

'Don't be so damn silly.' His voice was level. 'I would have been up there with you eight years ago. Shut up and go to bed.'

Freddy considered this. 'You'd have been there only at my invitation,' she said at last and fell silent. She had captured his attention fully now and held his gaze pensively. Finally, she said, 'You didn't answer my question, Joe.'

'Which one?'

'How you're going to get my butt off this couch.' She gave a deprecating smile.

'I'd give you a fireman's lift upstairs and dump you on the bed,' offered Joe, still repressed in tone, but Freddy thought she caught the slightest crease in the corners of his mouth.

'Ah ... I see. It would be a bit difficult, with the eiderdown as well. And I'd come down again. The thing is, it's darned cold up there, cold and lonely, and my feet are frozen.' She paused. 'I wondered if you'd like to warm them up for me.'

For what seemed an incredibly long time Joe just stood and regarded her, and she thought it wasn't going to work. Her heart began to thump, a wave of embarrassment sweeping over her. Then he moved slowly to her and knelt, pulling off the woollen socks and taking her feet into his lap, his hands massaging them with a regular rhythm, his eyes holding hers all the time.

Freddy swallowed hard, shivering as his hands made inroads along her calves. 'You see,' she said huskily, 'this warm room was very tempting...' Joe rose to his feet and brought her with him. He lifted her arms in the air and pulled off the T-shirt. '... and I thought, if you didn't mind...' She gave a gasp of pleasure as his hands moved over her bare flesh. '... just for tonight...'

Joe's mouth covered hers, stopping her breath. She sagged weakly against him and when his head lifted, he said with grim amusement, 'Shut up, woman, no need to underline everything. I understand the rules perfectly.' He was now shrugging off his own clothes, without haste, his eyes holding hers relentlessly.

Freddy began to tremble, but not with the cold, for she was consumed with a burning heat. The firelight played patterns, turning their flesh into a deep red-brown glow. Before Joe's hands were upon her, Freddy knew, remembered, sighed and offered herself to him, leaping ahead with her senses, as a torrent of joy roared through her. She was alive, soaring, singing to his music, caught and enraptured, yet free as a bird and flying; and then, and then, the wonderful fury was spent and she lay, fragile and exhausted against him.

She listened with curious detachment to their combined breathing. A log crackled in the grate, sending orange sparks shooting in all directions, colouring the room briefly. Joe made a movement as if to go and she said huskily, 'Don't!'

'I'm not,' he murmured, and reached out a hand and pulled the eiderdown over them, twitching a cushion from the chair and tucking it under her head to give her some portion of luxury that the hearth rug could not afford.

Freddy lifted her eyes to his face and found him gravely watching her. She said, 'Joe...' and his fingers touched her lips, stopping her.

He turned her over and wrapped himself against the length of her, ordering quietly, 'Hush, go to sleep, Frederica,' and to her surprise, she did.

Freddy woke to find herself alone under the eiderdown. The room was warm, the fire had been recently refuelled, and by the light coming through the curtains she could see that the clock said seven-thirty. She stretched and wriggled her toes and found she was wearing socks, which Joe had evidently pulled on for her. The thought made her smile and she lay in a snug cocoon and reflected sleepily that there was something to be said for living dangerously. What, she wondered, was Joe thinking now? Did he understand that she had come down to him on an impulse, that the motive governing that impulse was not clear to her? That nothing was changed?

She heard sounds coming from the kitchen, water gushing from the tap, the chink of a cup against a saucer, and she panicked. She leaped to her feet, grabbed her cast-off clothing, clutched the eiderdown round her and tiptoed hastily upstairs. She dressed quickly, shivering slightly in the cold atmosphere.

When she finally entered the kitchen Joe was pouring out coffee. He passed her a cup, saying calmly, 'Good morning. I've tuned in to the weather, snow is forecast for later in the day, but the morning should be clear. If we take it steady we should be OK.' He rinsed his cup under the tap and put it on the draining board. 'I'd like to get away as quickly as we can. I'm going round to try and start the car.'

'I'll clear up and leave the place tidy,' Freddy responded, grateful for his matter-of-fact tone and glancing at him properly for the first time. He was half-turned away from her, shrugging on the sheepskin coat. Stubble was showing on his chin making him look raffish, roughening his image, so that it was hard to reconcile this man with the one of a few hours ago... soft-voiced, with gentle, persuasive hands, loving. Perhaps it was just as well, she thought, watching him don scarf, ski hat and gloves.

'I won't be long,' Joe said crisply, going to the door. 'Keep your fingers crossed.'

Fifteen minutes later they were ready to leave. When Joe pulled the front door to, testing it with his hand to check that it was firmly secure, Freddy felt as though a door had been shut on more than the cottage.

Fate, however, was not finished with them yet. The journey to the hotel was slow and a little tense, and when they pulled into the car park Freddy, for one, heaved a sigh of relief.

'The main roads will be easier,' Joe said, as they left the Renault and went to their separate rooms.

Freddy showered, changed and packed her case. She carried it down to the car and as she approached she saw glass scattered on the surrounding snow. Coming nearer, her heart sinking

to her boots, she realised that between parking it
and now someone had smashed into the rear end.
She dropped her case and stood looking and could
have screamed with frustration and anger.

'Good God! What's happened?' Joe, coming up
from behind, his footsteps softened by the snow
underfoot, walked slowly round the Renault. He
took one look at her face and said, 'Come on, no
use standing here. Let's go and report it.' He took
the case from her unresisting hand and led her back
to the hotel.

So that was how Joe came to be sitting opposite
Freddy at her parents' dinner table in Boston that
evening, when he should have been back in
Queensbridge. She glanced across at him and
thought again how calmly he had taken the whole
incident. His raffish look was gone. He had
showered, shaved and changed and was obviously
enjoying her mother's cooking.

'I'm sorry Megan was in bed when you arrived,'
said Catherine Leigh. 'She tried to keep awake, but
in the end had to give in. More apple pie, Mr
Corey?'

'Thank you, no, that was delicious,' replied Joe.

'Do call him Joe, Mother,' urged Freddy.

'I shall do nothing of the kind,' reproved
Catherine. 'I shall call him Joseph,' and she turned
and gave him a smile.

'It's good of you to put me up like this, Mrs
Leigh,' began Joe.

'Nonsense,' said Edmund. 'The least we can do.
It was extremely good of you to bring Freddy home.

It would have been a tedious journey for her by train, trying to cope with presents and luggage.'

'Let's go into the sitting-room, shall we?' suggested Catherine, rising from the table. 'I shall be making coffee, and tea for my husband, Joseph. Which do you prefer?'

'Coffee, please,' replied Joe, holding the door open for her to pass through.

'What a good thing you were with Freddy when that child was born,' Catherine stated fervently. 'No doubt you would have managed on your own, darling, but it must have been reassuring to have Joseph there.'

'You can say that again,' joked Freddy, bringing in a tray of coffee things, and putting it on a low table near to where Joe was standing. She shot him a challenging glance as she added, 'But Marion wouldn't have been having her baby if Joe hadn't been with me.'

'My dear, what do you mean?' Catherine turned from her daughter's deadpan face to Joe's amused one in bewilderment.

'She means that I attract trouble,' Joe explained, 'but, in fact, it's the other way around, Mrs Leigh. My life is quite ordinary and free of incidents until I'm with Fred, and then anything can happen.'

'I see.' Catherine stilled, studying him intently, as if for the first time really seeing him. She nodded slightly and then recollected her manners. 'Do sit down, Joseph, unless you'd rather not after all that driving. Freddy, dear, where is your father?'

'I heard him say something about his pipe,' Freddy replied, and her mother left the room. She began to arrange the cups and saucers on the tray. It was strange, seeing Joe here in her parents' house, the house of her childhood. It was built of Lincolnshire stone, the house, and she loved it. The furniture was old and inherited from her father's people; good solid oak and mahogany, large sofas, ginger jars in Chinese blue and white, Chelsea and Worcester vases and plates, a grandfather clock that chimed the hour—all lovingly polished and cleaned.

'Do you know this area?' she asked, lifting her eyes to find Joe regarding her thoughtfully.

'I know Lincoln,' he replied, and Freddy sat back on her heels and chatted about her home county, Boston and its surroundings in particular. It was a subject she loved and knew well so it was easy for her. As she spoke she was thinking how futile it was to make plans. Right now, if she had had her way, Joe would have been back in Queensbridge, getting on with spending this pre-Christmas evening the way he wanted to, in the company of who knows? Instead of which he was here, with her.

'Are you sure it's convenient for me to stay overnight?' Joe asked suddenly. 'I can quite easily find an hotel. Do you want me to do that, Frederica?'

'Why should I?' she replied as calmly as she could, dropping spoons into saucers. 'And in any event, you won't be allowed to go.' She straightened as her father walked in. 'Daddy, if you're going to offer Joe a brandy, shall I get the glasses?'

Edmund, slightly distracted, nodded, patting his pockets. 'Your mother said—ah, here they are!' He set aside the curtain at the bay window and spied pipe and tobacco on the ledge. 'How am I expected to know that's where I'd left them when they're hidden?' he complained good-naturedly. 'Shouldn't, of course,' he added conspiratorially to Joe, who was watching him with amusement, 'but I only indulge at this time of the day. Do you mind?' When Joe shook his head, smiling, Edmund busied himself with pipe and pouch. 'You were lucky the mother was healthy and the birth a normal one. She was lucky, too.'

Freddy sank down in an armchair and wondered if Joe was getting fed up with the subject.

'Mind, that's how births should be, but things can go wrong. You, Freddy, were a contrary creature and caused a great deal of trouble.'

'Would you say I'd changed much, Dad?' teased Freddy, and her father smiled.

'Shall you keep in touch?' he asked, lifting his eyes above the flame of a match as he puffed at the pipe.

'They've asked us to be godparents,' explained Freddy. 'We paid them a quick visit in hospital before we left and found ourselves minor celebrities! Joe's namesake is very sweet.' She ran fingers through her hair, shaking her head in wonderment. 'We very nearly didn't go past their cottage. Do you know, the more I think about it, the more horrified I become.'

'That's often the case,' observed her mother, coming in and overhearing. 'It's been known for people to perform marvellous feats of courage with great calmness and then go completely to pieces afterwards.' She set the tea tray next to her husband and began to pour. She handed his cup to him and turned her attention to the coffee tray. 'Freddy, darling, two spoons in the saucer?' she commented drily, and removed one to its proper place. She then turned to Joe and asked, 'You haven't explained exactly what happened to the Renault.'

Joe shrugged. 'No one actually witnessed anything, but we suspect it was a brewery lorry on delivery that morning. It's possible the driver didn't know he'd done it, but that I personally doubt. He'd surely have heard the breaking glass.'

'We parked it in the hotel car park,' Freddy explained, 'and went to shower and change and pack. When I went out an hour later to load the car I found it smashed.'

Freddy sneaked a glance at Joe. He looked remarkably at ease in these surroundings, and was taking the change in his plans very much in his stride. He had driven her to Boston without any sign of impatience or irritation. She had protested loudly that it was too much of an imposition for him to drive her home, that it was miles out of his way, and Joe had merely stood and waited until she had run out of steam. Finally, she had lamely accepted his offer, although what she had really wanted to do was to fall on his neck in gratitude, but matter-of-fact coolness seemed to be the order of the day so she had restrained herself. Their journey, amazingly, had been quite tame. She had begun to think that they were marked down in some malevolent jester's book!

'Of course, Boston in Massachusetts came from our Lincolnshire Boston,' her mother was now saying. 'Some of the Pilgrim Fathers from the

Mayflower settled there and remembered their home town. It's an interesting place. When you have more time for a visit Freddy must take you round.' Catherine drained her cup and then looked at Joe, tilting her head reflectively. 'I'm sure I recognise Joseph's name from somewhere, and I don't mean from his books.'

Catherine's remark brought Freddy's eyes from Joe to her mother.

'Probably from way back, Mother,' she offered quickly, rising to her feet and making for the coffee pot. She raised her brows at Joe, asking silently if he wanted a refill. He held out his cup and she took it, looking him full in the face and finding amusement in the depths of his brown eyes, though his face was solemn enough.

'I was one of Fred's tutors, for my pains, during her training,' he offered with a drawl, and Freddy glared at him, wishing he'd kept quiet.

'Do tell me how you became involved in television,' asked Catherine.

While Joe obliged, Freddy wondered if her mother had finally recalled where she remembered Joe's name. Eight years was a long time and Freddy had been reticent about the whole affair, hugging it to her almost as if she had known it wouldn't last. Catherine had known she was involved with someone, of course, but when she had come to London the few times during that period, she had stayed at the small family hotel the Leighs always used on such occasions, and for some quite genuine reason had never met up with Joe. She had certainly known that her daughter was in love, really in love, for the first time. Would she connect that long-ago lover with Joe? Freddy hoped desperately that she wouldn't.

'Are you married, Joseph?' Catherine enquired and her husband murmured, 'You can always object to my wife's catechism, Joseph!'

But Joe replied, smilingly, 'I shouldn't dream of doing so, sir. Mrs Leigh has, I'm sure, the purest of motives.'

Freddy nearly choked on her coffee.

'Joseph and I understand each other,' reproved Catherine comfortably.

'I haven't managed to find anyone who could put up with me for very long, Mrs Leigh,' Joe admitted with dry humour. 'I've been told I'm not an easy person to live with,' and his eyes drifted over to Freddy, a sardonic gleam in their depths.

Freddy ignored him.

'You don't sound as though you've had the time,' joked Edmund, 'but after thirty-five years of married life, I can recommend it.' He smiled at his wife, who leaned over and patted his arm tenderly.

Freddy changed her mind and looked at Joe. He caught her eye, but his face told her nothing.

She joined her mother in the kitchen, leaving the two men talking, the brandy bottle between them.

'He's an interesting young man,' asserted Catherine pensively. 'Has a spiky mind.'

'Young man, indeed!' Freddy grinned. 'He'll be flattered. He's coming up for thirty-seven by my reckoning.'

Reappearing from the depths of the pantry carrying the Christmas cake, Catherine replied, 'When he was born I'd just met your father—that's young for me.' She put the cake on the work surface and opened cupboards for icing sugar and eggs. 'He has a well shaped head,' she offered irrelevantly, 'and nice ears. The shape of a person's ears can tell you a lot.' She paused and added, 'I told him I liked his writing, but not his views. He's too cynical for his own good.'

Freddy laughed, delighted. 'And what did Joseph say to that?'

Catherine separated the yolks from the whites and dropped the whites into the icing sugar. 'He said I shouldn't mix up the writing with the man, that they were separate, but he hasn't convinced me. I shouldn't have thought he was the self-destructive type, though.'

'No!' exclaimed Freddy, sardonically. 'Strong-willed and too bloody sure of himself is Joseph Corey.'

Catherine murmured, 'Language,' and a moment later added thoughtfully, 'No one can be totally invincible.'

Freddy made no comment. She wasn't sure of anything any more.

## CHAPTER SIX

FREDDY surfaced the next morning and lay in that hazy land of not being fully awake; she was snug and warm, smiling sleepily as she heard Megan chattering away, her voice revoltingly bright and cheerful. Two seconds later Freddy leaped out of bed, and dashed across the landing to stop on the threshold of the guest-room. The door was ajar.

Megan was sitting on the end of the bed in the lotus position. She was wearing pyjamas that were a little too short in the arms and legs—she was growing fast, thought Freddy in some surprise—and her hair stuck out at all angles. She was asking in a serious tone what Joe had put in his letter to Father Christmas.

The recipient of this question was sitting propped up by two pillows, arms folded across a bare chest. His eyes were fixed on Megan, but the movement at the door attracted his attention momentarily, and on seeing Freddy his brow quirked slightly, but he ignored her and replied gravely, 'I guess when you reach my age you have to take what's left over in the way of presents. Not much use writing.'

'Oh, but you must write,' Megan told him earnestly. 'Mummy always writes, we send our letters together. Mummy asked for a holiday in Florence—she's always wanted to go there—with Harrison Ford.' She hesitated briefly, explaining patiently,

'Indiana Jones,' and leaning forward, eyes narrowing, she added with growing interest. 'You look a bit like him.'

'I'm much better-looking than Indiana Jones,' objected Joe in a pained voice. 'I admit he might be in better shape.'

'*Megan*!' interrupted Freddy, wanting to laugh. 'What are you doing in here?'

Megan turned her head, undismayed. 'I wanted to see what he looked like.'

'But you're not supposed to disturb...'

'His name's Joseph,' supplied Megan, returning her gaze to Joe, 'like Mary and Joseph and baby Jesus, and he can't get out of bed because he hasn't any pyjamas on.'

Joe covered his eyes with one hand and Freddy controlled her mouth.

'And he hasn't written to Father Christmas.' The awfulness of this showed plainly in Megan's voice and on her solemn little face. 'Is it too late, do you think, Mummy? He comes tonight, doesn't he?'

Before Freddy could answer, Joe removed his hand and opened his eyes, saying simply, 'I don't think it would be much good, Megan. You see, I really need a Fairy Godmother. I don't think Father Christmas could manage what I want.'

'Joseph,' Megan whispered, hitching a few inches forward, 'what is it?'

'If you tell what you want, then you don't get it,' broke in Freddy hastily, not liking the glint in Joe's eyes. She walked across to the bed and plucked her daughter from it. 'We have to decorate the tree this morning, have you forgotten?'

'Hooray!' Megan beamed at the thought, ran to the door and then stopped. 'You can help, Joseph,' she told him kindly, and was gone.

There was silence for a moment while Freddy watched her daughter's comical form run down the landing to her own room. She then turned her attention to Joe and found he was smiling.

She said, 'I'm awfully sorry, Joe. Did she wake you?'

'No, I was about to make a move.' The smile deepened. 'She's a honey.'

Freddy found she was incredibly pleased. 'Yes, she is, isn't she?' She suddenly remembered she was wearing a shortie nightshirt and felt too exposed. She began to move to the door, glancing back innocently to ask, 'Do you think you can compete with Indiana Jones?' Laughter bubbled upwards. 'Not in such good shape indeed!' and when Joe flung back the covers to get out of bed she turned and fled, still laughing.

Joe helped decorate the tree, and when Megan learned he was then leaving she hid behind the sofa, never one to make a fuss in public. Joe, who had gone out to see if the Tiger would start, returned to say goodbye. Catherine indicated the sofa when he asked where Megan was and he crawled behind it, softly calling her name. Whisperings could be heard for some seconds and finally they both emerged. Tears had been wiped and Megan said with careful pride, 'Joseph and me have a secret.'

'How lovely,' Catherine said, smiling. Freddy made no comment, standing by the window, looking on. Megan took her granny's outstretched hand and submitted to her suggestion that she put on outdoor clothes so that she could wave goodbye to Joseph from the gate, and the two of them left the room.

Freddy had watched the performance behind the sofa with mixed feelings, and the fact that they were mixed added to her touchiness. She didn't want Joe anywhere near Megan if she had a choice. Yes, she knew it was irrational, but there it was, that was how she felt. She wanted him gone. He had been kind and extremely helpful, but now she wanted him to leave.

She said quickly, 'I can't thank you enough for bringing me home, Joe. I know you don't want any thanks, but you're going to have them all the same. I just hope it hasn't been too inconvenient and upset too many of your plans.'

Joe listened to her patiently and said, 'Tell me, Fred, what's so significant about two spoons in the same saucer?'

'What?' Caught off balance, Freddy wrinkled up her nose and then remembered the previous evening, taking coffee, and her mother remarking that there were two spoons in the same saucer— Freddy's doing. 'Oh, that!' She shrugged and gave a short laugh. 'Old wives' tale. It means a wedding will be on the way.' Her voice was drily amused.

'Does your mother believe in superstition?'

'I don't think so, generally. She would, however, like to see me married again, so you'd better watch out, Joe. I think she sees you as a likely candidate. But don't worry, I've already told her you're not the marrying kind.' As she spoke she was moving into the hall, Joe following. 'Have a good Christmas and take care on the journey home, won't you? I suppose I'll be seeing you around in the New Year.'

Joe made some reply and caught her arm. She turned, a questioning look on her face and heard him say, 'Too good to miss,' and she was enveloped in a firm embrace and very thoroughly kissed. As kisses went it couldn't reach the scale of ten, not having the time or place in its favour, but all things being equal, it couldn't be written off completely. Joe felt big and overpowering in the sheepskin, and when he lifted his head he was in no hurry to let her go. His eyes bored down into hers, a satirical gleam deepening the brown depths, and his lips were slightly pursed. What he might have said or done next Freddy was not to learn, for a movement out of the corner of her eye told her they had had witnesses. She gave a nervous jump and would have thrust him away, but Joe wouldn't let her.

'Me too, please, me too,' demanded Megan, running forwards and lifting her arms. Joe slowly released Freddy—no hurried, embarrassed leaping apart for him—and he grinned, picking Megan up with ease. He kissed both her cheeks, her forehead, her nose and finally her lips, in quick pecks. When he put her down, Megan urged, 'Now Granny! Your turn, Granny.'

'Don't you think I'm too old?' smiled Catherine.

Joe shook his head and held out a hand. 'No one's too old for mistletoe,' he stated firmly, and drew his hostess under the hanging twig of evergreen and kissed her on both cheeks, French fashion. He gave her another of his special smiles, warm and genuine, without a hint of the usual cynicism, thanked her again for her hospitality, and then took Megan's hand and they walked together down the path.

Catherine murmured, 'That young man has incredible charm, when he chooses.' She regarded her daughter thoughtfully. 'The word has gone out of fashion these days, but your father would know what I mean, and I use it as a compliment.' She returned her gaze to her granddaughter, who was still waving from the gate even though the red sports car could no longer be seen and could only just be heard, rumbling in the distance. 'Megan is starved of the company of men.'

Freddy gave a grim smile. 'I know, Mum, but there's not much I can do about it at the moment. Nothing sensible, I mean.' The smile trembled a little, and became vulnerable.

Catherine searched her daughter's face for some seconds and then touched her cheek, saying softly, 'I know, I know,' and went on more briskly, 'Shall we walk to the bakery? The exercise will do us all good, Dini especially.'

Freddy nodded and went to fetch her coat. She knew her mother was right, but nothing was perfect and life was mostly compromise. Some people had to compromise more than others, that was all.

On impulse she sought out a dictionary and flipped through until she came to the word she was seeking. Charm... quality of exercising fascination. She grimaced, shut the book and went to join her mother and Megan.

Christmas Day brought forth several gifts, and a few surprises. A parcel had come for Megan from her father in Hong Kong which, when opened, produced forth a number of presents suitable for a five-year-old. And there were two parcels under the tree from Joe, obviously sneaked there by him when no one was about. As Freddy watched Megan open hers she realised that he must have brought them with him from Queensbridge, for they were beautifully gift-wrapped and there had been no opportunity to buy anything in Yorkshire.

Megan opened up the paper with great excitement and found a large, beautifully illustrated book of fairy tales written by the Brothers Grimm. It was a little too old for her at the moment, but the pictures, some quite weird and menacing, others strange and beautiful, enchanted her, and nothing more was heard from her for some time as she turned the pages.

Freddy opened her parcel with an amount of restraint, aware of her parents' interested gaze. It was apparent by its shape that it, too, was a book, and when she pulled aside the wrapper she found it to be a hardback copy of Joe's first book. Written on the flyleaf was a simple inscription with no embellishments.

Freddy handed it to her mother, saying, 'I mentioned once that my copy had been lost—I lent it to someone and they never returned it, but said they had. It was then that I vowed I'd never lend out any more of my books.'

Catherine was reading the jacket-flap and murmured, 'My goodness, he wrote this when he was only twenty-two!'

'Read it over the holiday, Mum,' suggested Freddy.

Catherine passed the book to her husband, who said, 'Um ... nice chap, Joseph—interesting to talk to.'

Between the mouth of the Steeping River, pinnacled by Gibraltar Point, and the old market town of Boston, a twenty-three mile stretch of seabank lay between marshy foreshore and reclaimed fertile farmland. It was not frequented by holidaymakers in the summer months, they made for the sandy beaches of Skegness and Mablethorpe, seeing nothing to interest them in the mud-flats and marshes.

For the bird-watchers and wildlife enthusiasts it was a different matter, and for the Leigh family, the place was special. This remote shore held happy childhood memories for Freddy, and there was not one inch of its coastline that was not known to her. With friends she had sailed a dinghy, fished and swum, played games of hide and seek, shipwrecks and castaways, and as she had grown older she had inherited her parents' love of wild flowers and bird and animal life.

The day after Boxing Day, Edmund Leigh and his daughter, together with Houdini, drove the few miles to the coast, parked, and set off for a brisk walk along the shore.

'Will that hound come back?' Edmund asked curiously as the distance between them and Houdini increased.

Freddy grinned. 'With luck, he will! He's much better at coming to heel in open spaces than back home.'

As if to prove her point Houdini came pounding back, ran twice round them and set off again, Edmund muttering, 'Absolutely mad, that dog.'

Freddy tucked her arm through her father's and they began to walk. They were well wrapped up and their faces began to take on a healthy pink glow from the wind. Freddy swept her gaze across the waters of the Wash, dark grey merging into the lighter grey of the sky. Snow lay in patches on the mud-flats and spiky grass on the seabank struggled to give some colour to the landscape.

'I sometimes think,' she said, 'that nowhere has such huge skies as the Fens.'

Edmund grunted his agreement. They walked in a desultory manner for a while, faces slightly down against the head wind, and then he said suddenly, 'Your mother seems quite taken with your Joseph Corey.'

Freddy gave a short, hard laugh. 'I don't think Joe would agree with the possessive adjective, Dad, and neither do I.' She slanted her father a glance.

'Um ... well, of course, you know best, but as we've never heard anyone call you Fred before and get away with it, you can see why your mother and I had food for thought.' They walked a few yards in silence and he squeezed her arm. 'You don't have to talk about it if you don't want to,' Edmund said gently, and Freddy grimaced and gave a funny little shrug of her shoulders.

'There's hardly anything to tell, Dad. Life's full of surprises, isn't it? I suppose Mother remembered him. What a revoltingly good memory she has.'

'My dear girl, what happens to you is important to us.' Edmund stopped. 'Shall we turn back? I think we've gone far enough.'

They called to Houdini who stood watching them, wondering if they meant it, and when they began to walk away from him he ran after them, tongue lolling, mouth a wide grin.

The wind was now behind them, making it easier. A bird flew out of the marsh and disappeared inland.

Freddy asked diffidently, 'What do you know about Joe?'

'Not a great deal. The main thing being that at one time he was important to you.' Edmund paused and asked gently, 'Is he still?'

'Dad, it's eight years ago! A lot's happened since then.'

'Time doesn't mean much.'

'I don't know what I feel,' Freddy said bitterly, and kicked a lump of hard snow. 'I'm hardly an authority on love, am I?'

'There's no need to let one mistake colour your life. And it's better to acknowledge a marriage isn't working than carry on, with everyone being miserable. The problem is, we Leighs never like admitting we're wrong.' Edmund was glad to see that this produced a small smile.

'I'm no repressed female, Dad. I have my moments, but on my own terms.'

'And Corey is a threat to those terms?'

'He could be,' she replied simply. Conversation was halted as they reached the car. Houdini was caught and dried off and, as they settled into their seats, Freddy went on gruffly, 'I don't want you and Mum to worry about me.'

'Ah, well, that's difficult,' admitted Edmund, 'because, of course, we do. It's our privilege. Not that our concern for your future is out of proportion, you understand. We respect the way you're tackling living on your own, how you're bringing up Megan. We do what we can to help, but the reins are in your hands, which is how it should be. We won't be around for ever. The thing is, Freddy, my dear, we all have certain characteristics that work against us sometimes, and it's necessary to remember them from time to time. You have a tendency to expect too much from those you hold in esteem, those you love. You put them up on a pedestal and are devastated and hurt when they fall off. You also expect too much of yourself, which I suppose does even things out a little.' He gave a smile.

Freddy pulled a face. 'You make me sound like a fool, Dad.'

'No, no, it's not a bad fault, in fact it often produces remarkable results in those who aspire to live up to your expectations. But I think now you're veering the other way, and not expecting anything, and that would be a pity. Relax a bit, eh? Don't be so hard on yourself.' He took the hand nearest to him and squeezed it encouragingly. Then, voice changing to a brisk note, he went on, 'And now, if I've judged rightly, it will be sherry time when we get home!' Giving her a twinkling smile, he put the subject aside as they talked of other things on the way home.

Freddy finished Joe's book, reading in bed that night. She had forgotten how good it was, as it delicately explored an idyllic summer through the eyes of a group of adolescents before they stepped into adulthood. She lay back on the pillows, staring at the ceiling. Whenever she thought of Joe and their time together she remembered the fun and laughter, the spirited arguments, the wild, passionate lovemaking, and conveniently forgot the depths to the man, perhaps on purpose. She was glad she had given in to impulse and let him make love to her, the night of baby Josephine's birth. It was an incident in its own right, isolated, happening for many reasons, probably the most important one being that she needed to exorcise the wretched man.

She put down the book and turned out the lamp. It was not quite so easy to exorcise the mental picture of firelight playing on a smooth, rounded shoulder and hip, and the touch of magical hands...

Catherine drove them back to Queensbridge, and stayed a couple of days before returning to Boston. Judith was still in America and Mrs Mallory was not coming in until school started again, so Freddy was looking forward to having Megan to herself for the remaining few days left of the holiday. She was lucky to be able to borrow Judith's Mini while she waited for the Renault to be repaired.

Megan was consumed by the secret she shared with Joe, and could barely restrain herself from spilling it to her mother. Freddy had confused emotions about this secret. She didn't want to be linked with Joe in any way, yet remembered her mother's comment that Megan was starved of male company. And Megan was so excited about it—whatever it was—that Freddy hadn't the heart to do anything about stopping it.

The Tiger pulled up outside the house one morning and Megan came rushing into the kitchen, shouting, 'Mummy, Joseph's come! It's about my secret!'

Freddy groaned a sigh. She had no make-up on, was in her oldest pair of jeans with a well-washed baggy sweater, and her hair was tied back with one of Megan's ribbons. Not, she told herself grimly as she brushed flour from her hands, that it was necessary for her to look glamorous for Joe. She left on the butcher's apron; after all, she was cooking and it was a good cover-up.

It was snowing again and flakes were clinging to Joe's hair and to shoulders made broad by the sheepskin coat. A flurry of wind hurled snow into the hall and he stepped in quickly.

'Hello, Joe,' Freddy said, 'nice weather you've brought with you. Let me have your coat.' She waited while he shrugged it off and hung it over the banister. She made herself meet his eyes with a clear, friendly look and received a similar one in return. The earlier excitement of Joe's arrival was now gone and Megan gazed up at him, tongue-tied. He bent his knees and brought himself down to her level.

'Hello, Meggie. Did Father Christmas come?'

Megan nodded shyly. 'You can thank Joseph for his present now, can't you, Meg?' primed Freddy, who knew how successful that particular gift had been by the number of times she had been obliged to read it. Megan needed no second bidding and then asked if she could kiss him, please?

'I would be disappointed if you didn't,' replied Joe, whereupon Megan put the palms of her hands against his cheeks and gave him a solemn kiss. Joe scooped her up and straightened, asking, 'Is flour in fashion these days, Fred?' and lightly brushed the dusting of white powder from her chin.

Megan chuckled delightedly and Freddy said, 'Of course it is, fancy you not knowing. Would you like coffee?' and preceded him into the kitchen. She nodded to the coffee pot keeping hot on the hob. 'Help yourself, I want to get this pie in the oven,' and she began to roll out the pastry. Joe put Megan back on her feet, unhooked a mug from the dresser and poured himself coffee, his eyes sweeping across the variety of cakes and pastries cooling on the side.

'I can't remember such domesticity in the old days,' he mused. 'What hidden talents you do have, Frederica.'

'Any idiot can cook,' Freddy came back sweetly, 'even you!' She dropped pastry over the dish of meat and vegetables, catching Joe's brief look of amusement before she expertly crimped the edges.

'Ah, but a woman's place is in the kitchen,' he responded, face deadpan, 'and far be it from me to deny her the privilege and delight it gives to bake for her one and only true love.'

'The temptation to hit you over the head with this rolling pin is extremely great,' remarked Freddy pleasantly, 'but I'll resist because I'm trying to teach Meg that violence is a last resort. She's of an age, unfortunately, to be included in the category of enslaved female—Michael Carlyon being the culprit— but I hope to educate her. By the time she's in the position of becoming some man's mate I trust she will be able to hold her own with a screwdriver and sparking plugs and tell him to cook his own goose. However, at the moment she would be thrilled, really thrilled, if you would succumb to the temptation of tasting one of her jam tarts.'

Megan clapped her hands, exclaiming, 'Joseph, you must have one, but the jam might be too hot. Will the jam be all right, Mummy?'

'The jam will be just perfect,' assured Freddy, her face overly innocent, and watched as Joe, with due ceremony, popped one of the tiny tarts into his mouth. From past experience Freddy knew the pastry would be rock-hard, having been rolled out many times with frowning concentration.

'Dee-lishous!' proclaimed Joe, chomping manfully.

'Do have another,' urged Freddy with gentle persuasion.

'I shall take two,' declared Joe, and did so, sampling them with every evidence of enjoyment, while Megan looked on, her eyes shining with pride.

'You're a brave man, Joseph Corey,' Freddy murmured, for his ears alone. Then, turning to Megan, went on normally, 'Why don't you show Joseph your doll's house, Meggie?' She turned to the sink and began to wash her hands, while Megan pulled at Joe, leading him out of the kitchen.

Freddy leaned against the sink, her heart thumping loudly in her ears. She would have to keep away from him, have to! For a split second, watching him with Megan, she had imagined Joe being with them always, imagined a swift succession of scenes, similar to the one they had just played, the three of them having fun, teasing and laughing and sharing, and she had had to turn away before Joe could read her thoughts, catch the longing in her eyes. He had no right to be so good with children, she thought despairingly, it just wasn't fair! Why was he bothering with Megan like this? Her mind darted to and fro, choosing and rejecting answers. She gave an exasperated sigh and pushed the pie in the oven. As she was doing so Megan rushed in, excited, and flung herself at her mother. Joe followed and leaned against the door-frame, looking on, a small secret smile on his lips, his eyes on Freddy, his manner lazy.

He drives the right car, Freddy thought suddenly, seeing the gleaming red Tiger in her mind's eye. He's like a tiger himself, lazily waiting, dozing in the sun until it's time to pounce.

She hushed Megan's waterfall of words and, picking her up, sat her on the kitchen table. 'Slowly, Meggie darling, slowly. If you talk so fast I can't understand what you're trying to tell me. Joseph wants to take you where?'

'To see Peter Pan fly. It was our secret. You can come too, Mummy. Joseph says so.'

Freddy looked over her daughter's head and met Joe's look. 'At Drury Lane?' she questioned. 'When?'

'On Saturday, if it's convenient.'

'We can go, Mummy, can't we?' begged Megan, beginning to be worried that such a marvellous treat might be denied her.

'We could be doing something else on Saturday,' challenged Freddy, hating herself, knowing she could never say no to the treat, for Megan's sake.

'Your mother assured me that you would be free,' Joe responded equably.

'How organised you are, Joe. So Mother's been in on the act too? Yes, she did ask me to keep this Saturday free in case they came over.'

Megan tugged her sleeve. 'Can we go, Mummy?'

'Yes, we can go,' Freddy answered, lifting her daughter from the table and watching her dash excitedly into the hall, Houdini barking at her heels. 'It's very kind of you, Joe.' Her thanks sounded stilted even to her ears, and she made more effort. 'I had tried to get tickets myself but couldn't.'

'It's a case of who you know.'

'What would you have done if Mother's little plan hadn't worked?'

'I had every faith in Mrs Leigh.'

You must have made Mother's day, thought Freddy with grim amusement.

'And if you couldn't have made it, I would have asked Nina to come with us—with your permission, of course. Nina's good with children,' Joe said blandly.

Over my dead body, thought Freddy. 'I haven't thanked you for my Christmas present, Joe.'

His lips twitched. 'I know you haven't. Thanking me doesn't come easy, does it, Fred?'

'I've hardly had the opportunity to get a word in,' she defended, annoyed to feel the colour rise in her cheeks. Blast the man, he was too perceptive for words! 'And written thanks are in the post.' Thank goodness she was able to say that. 'After all, it is Megan you came to see, isn't it?'

Joe inclined his head, eyes dancing. 'I fear I'm rapidly falling in love with your daughter, Fred.'

'Poor Joe, at the mercy of a female!' she mocked. 'Never mind, I'm sure you'll soon recover. And as for your book, I'm delighted to have a copy again, and one signed by the author too! I've re-read it and enjoyed it even more than the first time. Thank you.'

'Megan thanked me properly,' he pointed out silkily.

Freddy had the mental picture of Megan's hands on Joe's cheeks as her serious little face came close for the kiss.

'Meggie is given to impulsive gestures,' she told him, and walked into the hall to retrieve his coat. 'What are the arrangements for Saturday?'

She resisted the pleas of Megan to join her at the window to wave goodbye. What the devil had she let herself in for? she wondered, and what else could she have done? Certainly Nina Welsh wasn't going to have the pleasure of seeing Meggie enjoying her first *Peter Pan*! Really, she was beginning to feel that she had no control over anything any more! She would get Saturday over and done with, and then any further suggestions of outings for Megan would be firmly squashed. A warning smell issued from the kitchen and, giving a wail of alarm, she dashed to the oven and rescued the pie. Megan assured her mother, who seemed unusually upset, that she liked the 'burny-bits'.

Saturday arrived at last. The snow had turned to rain and Joe stowed wellies, raincoats and hats into the car boot without comment. He raised brows at the holdall and Freddy said drily, 'Travelling with a five-year-old has its hazards and there are some things a wise parent never goes without.'

Joe grinned and secured Megan into the back.

Though it rained solidly for the whole of the day, it was one of pure magic. Megan sat riveted in the theatre, wide-eyed throughout the play, tears very close when it was thought that Tinkerbell was dying, cheering when Captain Hook was overthrown, completely lost in the world of make-believe. Freddy, watching Joe watching Megan, wished she understood him.

They had high tea after the show and Megan had known, young as she was, that this was a special treat and behaved beautifully. Freddy, like Megan, didn't want the day to end.

It was past Megan's bedtime by the time they arrived back at Dean Close. Joe carried her in, fast asleep, and while he was unloading the car Freddy undressed her and put her into bed. When she was settled, Freddy found Joe in the living-room, rain glistening on his trenchcoat and the soft felt hat he had removed on entering.

Would he stay for a while? Freddy wondered, her pulse quickening despite all her good intentions. She was saved from wondering for long by the ringing of the telephone. She excused herself and went into the hall to answer it and returned, saying, 'It's Nina Welsh, for you.'

He was not long. Coming back into the room, he explained, 'I gave Nina your number. I hope you didn't mind?'

'Not at all,' Freddy said. 'I'm sorry Megan isn't awake to thank you herself for such a lovely day, but I think you must know how much she enjoyed it. It was kind of you to take her. To take us. I've enjoyed myself immensely.'

'Me too.' Joe smiled. 'I haven't seen *Peter Pan* for years, and Meggie was a worthy excuse. Goodnight, Frederica.'

Freddy closed the door on him and slipped the chain. What a fool she was! She had only herself to blame. Admittedly life had been giving a few malicious little digs, throwing her into Joe's path willy-nilly, undermining her intention to keep out of his way. And she had given in to an impulse up in Yorkshire, which she didn't regret one little bit, but now was the time to take stock, to realise and accept her vulnerability where he was concerned.

She made herself a stiff drink and sat down to watch a soporific soap on the television. When the front doorbell rang she was surprised and went to answer it, finding Patrick Tyson standing under the porch.

'Why, hello, Patrick,' she exclaimed, 'what brings you here?'

'I was passing and stopped on the off chance you might be in.' Patrick stepped inside, smoothing his fair hair with the palm of his hand. 'But there is a reason for the visit,' he added.

Unbidden, Joe's words about Patrick regarding herself shot into Freddy's mind and she squashed the prickle of unease she had felt on seeing her boss. To hell with Joe's snide remarks, and as she had told him in no uncertain manner—she could look after herself.

'Can I get you a drink? Whisky?' she asked, switching off the TV.

'Thanks.' Patrick followed her into the room. She was used to seeing him in suits, so the casual waterproof jerkin and sweater and cavalry twill trousers were unfamiliar to her. He really was extremely handsome, and his eyes were the deepest blue she had ever seen on a man. She wondered why he didn't attract her in the least.

'A whisky and dry ginger coming up.' Freddy handed him the glass and topped up her own. 'Did you have a good Christmas, Patrick? And how is Dinah?'

'She's well. We don't set much store by Christmas, you know. Cheers, by the way. We had one or two parties, sorry you were away and missed them, and we were back in the office by the Wednesday.' He smiled. 'I suppose you had a traditional Christmas with your family?'

Freddy nodded and smiled back. 'I think that's the way it's going to be for years,' she admitted warmly. 'Children become secure knowing what to expect, and to tell the truth, we adults love it too.'

'I heard about the trouble you had with your car from Corey. A damned nuisance, that. When is it going to be ready?'

When had Joe seen Patrick? At one of those parties, perhaps? 'They said next Tuesday,' said Freddy.

'I have an appointment in Leeds on Tuesday. I can give you a lift up.'

'Oh, well, that's kind of you, Patrick, but...'

The doorbell saved her from floundering any more. She rose thankfully to her feet, still carrying her glass, saying, 'It's quite a night for visitors... excuse me, Patrick.'

Joe was standing on the step, collar upturned, the brim of his hat pulled down low over his forehead, dripping the occasional drop of rain.

He was the last person she had expected and Freddy said in surprise, 'Why, hello again, Joe! What's the matter, have you forgotten something?' She gazed at him in puzzlement and wondered why his face looked so wintry.

'I found this in the car and thought Megan might be disappointed to find it missing in the morning when she wakes.' He handed her the *Peter Pan* souvenir programme which was full of glossy, coloured pictures of the artists and the show. He glanced over his shoulder towards Patrick's distinctive white Mercedes Benz parked at the kerb. 'Is Tyson here?'

Freddy stiffened at his tone. 'Yes. He's called in for a drink,' she replied smoothly, indicating her own glass, her chin coming up, resentful anger bringing a spark to her eyes.

'I see.' Joe stared at her hard, face wooden. 'I'm sorry I disturbed you.' He turned and walked down the path to the Tiger and Nina Welsh who was sitting in the passenger seat.

'Bloody-minded man!' ground out Freddy. 'Jumping to all the wrong conclusions!'

When she walked back into the room, she said with rather more enthusiasm than she intended, 'Thanks for the offer, Patrick, I'd love a lift.'

'Good.' Patrick rose to his feet and gave her a smile. He put down his empty glass. 'Thanks for the drink.' He followed her into the hall, ignoring Dini, who was wanting some fuss. 'I'll let you know more details about Tuesday later. Goodnight, Freddy.'

'Goodnight, Patrick.' Freddy closed the door behind him and thought angrily that it was all Joe Corey's fault!

# CHAPTER SEVEN

THE hotel dining-room was quiet and select, and the cuisine exemplary. Patrick, in a light-coloured suit, perfectly matched his surroundings. He was used to such creature comforts and it showed. In deference to the white Mercedes, Freddy was wearing a smart, long-jacketed navy suit with emerald-green accessories. This included a stylish trilby hat, set at a jaunty angle, which turned the eyes as she passed.

They had reached the coffee stage of the meal, and so far had spoken only of business matters. When Patrick had picked Freddy up that morning she had been regretting her impulsive acceptance of his offer of a lift, yet what excuse could she have given? No one without an extremely good reason would turn down a comfortable, relaxed ride in a Mercedes Benz! If Joe hadn't been so stupidly disapproving at finding Patrick at Dean Close she might have thought up something that would have sufficed, but he had made her so hopping mad she had said yes.

'I have some good news,' Patrick announced, 'we've been given the go-ahead from Finance for the Queen's project.'

'That's wonderful!' exclaimed Freddy, her face lighting up. So much had happened since she had first put the idea to Patrick that it had been pushed to the back of her mind and it must have been at least nine weeks ago.

'It's likely that more than one director will be involved over the eight or nine months' shoot,' Patrick paused and spooned sugar into his coffee, smiling as he went on, 'but I would like you to produce the programme, Freddy.'

A swoosh of pleasure swept over her, deepening the colour in her face. This was a prestigious undertaking. She tried to compose her voice, but could not totally hide her exultation. 'Thank you. I'm flattered you think me capable.'

'No need to be. You've proved yourself over the past three years.'

'When do we start?'

'The beginning of May, in time for the Shakespeare rehearsals, although we'll probably go in earlier for the preliminary casting and read-through. David Herrick is free at that time, so he'll be the first of the directors.'

Freddy nodded, pleased it was David, whose work she admired. She was already turning over in her mind possible snags that would need to be ironed out, although the Queen's Theatre, being based in Queensbridge, would mean she would be based at home for most of the time. The June trip to France for *Othello* could cause problems, but she would cross that bridge when it came. Possibly her mother would come over to Dean Close for that period—it would only be for a week—her father too, now that he was semi-retired.

Another aspect of the job that suddenly flashed through her with jolting vigour was that she would be coming into contact with Joe. He was directing *Othello* and, as producer of film to be shot inside the rehearsal rooms, following the play on stage and then on tour, she was bound to be bumping into him all the time. So much for keeping out of his way, she thought grimly.

She came back to what was going on around her with the realisation that Patrick had said something to her and that she had been slowly stirring her coffee for longer than was necessary.

She gave a laugh. 'Sorry, Patrick, I was miles away!'

'About seventy, I suspect, centring on the Queen's Theatre,' Patrick replied, smiling. 'I'm not complaining. I like to see hard work going hand in hand with talent.' He paused, as if searching for the right words. 'I admire you very much, Freddy, do you know that?'

Freddy gazed across the table, her face showing nothing of the alarm that now filled her. 'Why, thank you, Patrick, I'm very grateful for all your help and encouragement...'

'I wasn't talking about your work, although that does apply. You know what I really mean, don't you, Freddy?'

'I was trying to head you off,' Freddy replied quietly.

'Must you? There was no appointment in Leeds.' Patrick took the hand resting near his coffee cup in his. 'Didn't you guess?'

Freddy shook her head, her eyes on that hand clasp. She said, frowning slightly, 'If I'd known, I would have refused your offer.'

'I knew that.' Patrick released her hand which had lain in his passively, and sat back in his chair. 'Do you mind if I smoke?' When Freddy murmured, 'Please do,' he lit a cigarette and drew on it deeply before continuing, 'If it's Dinah you're thinking about, you wouldn't be hurting her. We go our own way these days. I won't bore you with the reasons.'

'I'm sorry, Patrick.'

'And I'd make sure we were discreet. I've held off from telling you how I feel for some time. It was never my intention to become emotionally involved with you, Freddy, but these things have a habit of creeping up unawares, and my good intentions collapsed, I'm afraid.' He studied her for a long moment. Freddy did not realise that she had lost her colour and that her green eyes were dulled with anxiety. 'I'm going to be disappointed, aren't I?' Patrick said at last.

'I'm sorry, Patrick.' Freddy felt like a stuck needle on a record, but couldn't think of anything else to say. She could hardly tell him he was a fool if he thought Dinah wouldn't find out. She probably suspected something already, Freddy thought, recollecting the smiling but cold manner Dinah always presented her way. And if Dinah's heart wouldn't be hurt, her pride certainly would be affected. There was something else she couldn't tell him—that she didn't fancy him.

Patrick glanced round the emptying dining-room, face impassive, returning to regard Freddy once more. 'Tell me, is David Herrick one of the reasons?' He grimaced a smile. 'Sorry, I shouldn't have asked that.'

Freddy shook her head slightly, putting an elbow on the table and pressing the tips of slender fingers on her forehead. 'David is a good friend and I like working with him.'

'But there is someone else?'

She dropped her eyes to her coffee, which looked revoltingly cold. 'Yes,' she heard herself saying, 'there is someone else.'

'Thank you for telling me. The dent in my ego is now not so deep.' Patrick's voice was wry. 'I won't embarrass you again, Freddy, and this alters nothing in our professional capacity. I want you to understand that.' He glanced at his watch. 'Shall we be going, if you've finished? We've still a few miles ahead of us.'

Freddy thought Harrogate beautiful, an attractive elegant city, noted for its waters and healthy, bracing air. The Renault was ready for collection, and while Freddy settled up the paperwork Patrick stood by the white Mercedes, waiting.

When she drove out of the garage and pulled up alongside, winding down the window, he said, 'Off you go. Drive carefully. There's someone I can see in Bradford. I've just rung them and they're in.' He smiled, nodded, and waved her on.

Freddy drove south with much to think about.

Judith, now back from America, showed no surprise when told about Patrick's declaration. 'Why shouldn't he fancy you? You're an attractive, intelligent woman, and if his home life isn't all it should be, you can understand why he's always at the office. I'm surprised he didn't guess you'd turn him down.'

'He did, but decided to ask anyway. I let him think there was someone else. It seemed kinder than saying I couldn't return the compliment.'

'That reminds me, how is Joseph Corey these days?' Judith's face was all innocence. 'Megan seems to have taken a shine to him, it's Joseph this and Joseph that.' She settled herself more comfortably in the chair. 'I turn my back and all sorts of things happen. Come on, fill me in.'

Freddy did so, in a matter-of-fact voice, telling Judith how Joe had taken over from Tiny Dakin in Yorkshire, how they had delivered baby Josephine together, how her car had been smashed and he had delivered her and her parcels to Boston, and finally the trip to *Peter Pan*.

Judith listened, making a few startled exclamations as the tale unfolded, asking no awkward questions, but reading much between the lines. At the end she said bluntly, 'Have you considered that Joe might be jealous of Patrick Tyson?'

'He has no right to be!' protested Freddy with quick anger.

'Don't be a fool, Freddy. Right doesn't come into it. Any idiot knows that.' She stretched and rose to her feet. 'I shall have to meet the guy. According to Megan he's some kind of cross between Father Christmas, He-Man and Indiana Jones.'

'Megan's opinion isn't to be trusted—she's a pushover for anything in trousers,' retorted Freddy darkly.

Freddy walked into Adam's office some days later, expecting to find the Queen's artistic director sitting behind his desk. For a moment she thought the place empty and was about to leave, thinking she had made a mistake, when a figure unfolded itself from a chair in the corner and moved into the light. It was Joe.

'Oh, I'm sorry, I was told...' began Freddy.

'That Adam was here? He asked me to apologise and could he see you this afternoon instead, at three, if that's convenient?' Joe hitched himself on the desk and folded his arms, regarding her dispassionately. 'There are some things we can go over together, details that need confirming, so we might as well do it now.' He pulled a chair over, indicating for Freddy to sit, and moved round the desk to sit in Adam's swivel chair. He poured a plastic beaker of water from the water-cooler, offering it to Freddy. When she shook her head he drank, lashes fanning his cheeks as he held his head back. He looked, thought Freddy sourly, as though he could do with both a shave and a haircut, and there were dark shadows under his eyes. They had not met since the evening of *Peter Pan*, although Freddy had caught sight of him around the theatre, and she had the feeling he had been avoiding her. Well, that suited her. She still deeply resented his implied criticism of Patrick's presence at her house that night—God knew what his imagination ran to! Even though events since had proved him right, there was also the inference that she could be swayed by Patrick's interest in her, and it was that which rankled the most.

'Who is your director?' asked Joe.

Freddy opened up her briefcase and brought out a folder full of information she had collated on the Queen's project and spread the pages on the desk.

'David Herrick,' she replied, her voice as cool and as even as his own. 'You remember him, perhaps, from the *Tandy* set?' An inner visual picture of David and Joe shaking hands suddenly hit her. How long ago was it? An incredible four months!

'Yes, I remember him.' Joe crushed the beaker and tossed it through the air into the waste basket. He then began to ask a number of pertinent questions about times and dates, and noted them down in a memo book as Freddy supplied the answers. 'I think that's all for now.' Joe closed the notebook and fitted the cap back on to his pen. He went on bluntly, 'I want to get one thing straight. I'm quite happy for your company to film here, so long as you don't get in my way.'

Well, really! thought Freddy in disgust. What does he think we are, amateurs? She replied pleasantly, 'That's understood, of course, and we accept that we must work round you. There's bound to be a certain amount of inconvenience—cables and suchlike—but we'll do our best to make it minimal. If you have any complaints you must come to me.'

'I shall, never fear.'

Really, the man was like a bear with a sore head today! Holding on to her temper, Freddy asked, 'Perhaps you could let me have your schedule for rehearsals?'

Joe slipped two foolscap sheets across the desk. 'This is it.'

'Thank you. We shall be going to London for the casting sessions. I have the date and venue written down somewhere.' She paused. 'Is there anything more you want to discuss?'

'I don't think so.'

Freddy began to collect her things.

'You fetched the Renault without any difficulty?' His face was wiped clean of any expression. 'I understand Tyson drove you there.'

Freddy's hands stopped their task and she looked up, a challenging spark in her eyes. 'Yes, he did,' she retorted, and gave him a brilliant smile. 'Wasn't I lucky?' The last of the papers were in the case. 'If there's anything else, you know where I am.' Giving him an efficient nod of the head she stalked out of the office. As she marched down the corridor she was thinking, how the hell did he find that out? And then, so what?

Tiny Dakin returned to the set of *Wuthering Heights*, a tall, thin, laconic individual, hobbling around with his leg in plaster. They worked hard at the studio, and when spring was teasing its way into new leaf and blooms Freddy and Tiny, together with cast and crew, journeyed north to finish off the outside location scenes. It seemed strange returning to the King's Head at Kettlewell without snow and Joe.

Freddy found the time to visit Marion and Colin, bearing gifts for the baby, and found them all well. Marion handed Josephine to Freddy to hold, and Freddy thought the baby had a better claim to being called beautiful now than she had when Freddy had last seen her. At eleven weeks old she was smiling and cooing and was gorgeous.

'Joseph came the other weekend,' Marion remarked, her voice warm. 'He's a very caring person, but, of course, you know that without me having to tell you.'

Freddy murmured something suitable and promised to sort out a date for the christening, one that would suit both Joe and herself. She handed Josephine over, saying with a grin, 'Here, take her, quick, I'm beginning to feel maternal and might sneak off with her!'

By the beginning of April everything was shot and edited, words dubbed, music and graphics added. At the end of the first run-through, Tiny leaned forward along the row of seats in the projection room and gave Freddy the thumbs-up sign. Freddy allowed herself to return the gesture, smiling, feeling quite pleased herself.

Easter was looming on the horizon and Megan arrived home one day carrying a huge Easter egg in a brightly coloured box, tied with a huge ribboned bow. Judith, who had picked Megan up from school, was looking smug.

'My goodness, where's that come from, Meggie?' asked Freddy, startled by the obvious expensiveness of the egg.

Judith put a hand over Megan's mouth, saying, 'I was standing by the Mini, waiting for the kids to come out, when this magnificent, hunky man strolled up to the gates, having first, I might add, unfolded himself from the depths of a snazzy sports car, an eye-catching red, that any self-respecting female would give her last pair of false eyelashes to have a ride in. When Meggie ran up to him as though he was God's gift, and was lifted up and given a hug, I said to myself, Judith, you can have one guess who that is.'

'It was Joseph, Mummy,' explained Megan indulgently, her voice indicating—Who else could it have been?

'I see,' replied Freddy, trying to ignore her daughter's glowing face and the mischievous light in Judith's eyes. Megan carried the egg carefully out of the room, telling Houdini sternly not to bump her.

Judith said airily, 'He came over and introduced himself. Shook my hand and smiled. He has a lovely smile, hasn't he?' She paused and tilted a look at her friend, adding thoughtfully, 'Do you think he's courting the mother through the daughter, Freddy?'

Her voice rising with incredulity, Freddy exclaimed, 'You do talk some rubbish, Ju! Courting implies marriage, and Joseph Corey doesn't believe in it. I admit he might want to get me into his bed, but that's something else altogether, and I'd probably have to join the end of the queue.' She paused. 'On second thoughts, the vibes I've been getting lately from him are distinctly anti. He thinks I'm having an affair with Patrick Tyson.' She returned her attention to her income tax return form, signalling the end of the subject.

Later that week she bumped into Joe in the public library. He hadn't seen her and she hesitated before walking over to where he was browsing through the biography section.

'Hello, Joe,' she said quietly.

Joe stilled, remained for a moment with his back to her and then swung slowly round to face her. 'Hello, Fred.' There was nothing much to read from the expression in his eyes, but at least they didn't freeze her on the spot.

'I wanted to thank you for Meg's Easter egg. She won't eat it, though, she says it's too pretty.'

Joe gave a lop-sided grin. 'Just tell her that chocolate loses its taste after a time, that should do it.' He raised a brow. 'Is there something else?'

Freddy said, 'I want you to stop giving her presents.'

'Why?' drawled Joe, eyes turning shrewd.

'Because...' The words that she had rehearsed so many times flew out of her head.

'... you hate to be beholden to me for anything.'

Freddy checked herself, remembering they were in the hushed quietude of the library. Some of the regulars, who knew her, were already glancing their way. 'That's not true. I don't want to sound ungrateful, but Megan's getting very fond of you, and I don't want her to get hurt.'

Joe's eyes narrowed, face darkening. 'Why should I hurt her, Fred?'

'Children never think things change, at least, not Meg's age. You'll go away and I couldn't expect you to remember her...'

'Your problem, Frederica,' Joe said with silky softness, 'is that you don't expect enough.' He paused. 'And who says I'm leaving?' He shot the book he was holding back into its place on the shelf. 'Does that bother you?'

'What you do, Joe Corey, is of no interest to me whatsoever, just as long as it doesn't involve my daughter.'

'Jealous, Fred?'

She stared at him, turned on her heel and swept out of the library, wondering why it always ended up with her wanting to throw something at him.

She called in at the Carlyons on her way home and found that Liz had sprained her wrist, falling from a chair. 'My own stupid fault, of course, and I've been duly scolded by Adam,' Liz confessed. She held out her bandaged wrist. 'Good job it's my left hand. I hope you've called in to say you're coming tomorrow evening. I'm not cancelling it just for this.'

'Lizzie, I'm sorry, but I can't get a sitter. I've tried all my trusty faithfuls. The family a few doors down are in quarantine, Judith has a meeting, and two others who are sometimes available are both doing something...'

'No problem,' Liz declared airily. 'Send Meggie to school tomorrow with her night things, and I'll pick her up with Michael. She can sleep here and go to school with us the next day.' Liz dived to rescue her young daughter from a precarious position on a chair, and gave her a noisy kiss on her plump cheek.

'But are you sure you want to be bothered?' asked Freddy dubiously. 'I mean, having another child in the house, as well as cooking for a dinner party?'

'Now you know I have help,' soothed Liz, 'and Megan, believe me, is no trouble. That's settled.' And it seemed it was.

To Freddy's surprise Nina Welsh was not one of the guests at the Carlyons' dinner party. She had had no idea who would be there, but when she saw the Tiger in the drive she had automatically expected to see Nina, too. The Tysons' Mercedes was also parked outside and when Freddy was placed at the dining-table, she wondered what Joe was thinking, finding himself partnered, rather obviously, with herself.

Patrick was always good company, and Dinah too seemed to be more relaxed than usual, possibly because of the warm, welcoming atmosphere created by Liz and Adam. Soon Freddy forgot about Nina, and Joe's feelings, and began to enjoy herself. After dinner she went upstairs to look in on the children. Michael was on the top bunk-bed and Megan underneath, both fast asleep. Victoria, or Plum, as Michael insisted on calling his sister, was flat on her stomach in her cot, also asleep. How lovely they looked, thought Freddy, and stifled any ongoing dreams.

As she walked into the long sitting-room, a beautiful room with windows at either end, now covered with deep rose curtains, talk was turned to the French tour of *Othello* in June.

'Lovely, lovely Beaugency and lovely, lovely France,' Liz was enthusing, her eyes shining at the thought.

'Remind me where Beaugency is?' requested Dinah.

'It's the next town of note on the Loire, after Orléans, going west,' offered Adam.

'It's a beautiful medieval city,' Liz went on, 'with one of those incredible bridges across the river that's so typically French, full of arches in pale-coloured stone.'

'We were lucky to be accepted for the Festival,' said Adam, handing round the balloon glasses of brandy while Liz dispensed the coffee. 'It's held in June every year in the courtyard of the Château de Dunois...'

'Built in the fifteenth century by the Bastard of Orléans,' added Liz, 'who, if you're hot on history, you'll remember was the companion-of-arms to Joan of Arc. It's a folk museum now.'

'I've just received confirmation,' said Freddy, taking a seat and smiling her thanks as she accepted a glass of Cointreau liqueur from her host, 'that we can film there.' The news was received with satisfaction by the Tysons and Carlyons, although Joe seemed barely to be listening, staring down into his brandy.

'You're going to come over, aren't you, Dinah?' asked Liz, and Dinah raised her dark, shapely brows.

'Try and stop me. As Patrick's chosen to direct the *Othello* filming himself...'

Joe's head came up, eyes sharp. 'I thought David Herrick was directing.'

'He is,' confirmed Patrick, leaning an arm against the mantel and addressing Joe thoughtfully, 'over here, but not in France. He's committed to something else in June, so I thought I'd put my director's hat on. I like to, every now and again.'

Was it Freddy's imagination or did Patrick's smile seem to be slightly challenging as he directed it at Joe? This piece of information was news to her, too, and she hoped she had kept her face from showing it to the others. As the talk went on Freddy found she was on the receiving end of a number of speculative, thought-provoking glances from a certain pair of judging brown eyes. It began to get on her nerves.

'So, as Adam is half-French, we naturally have relations and friends in most parts of France,' Liz was saying, 'and the poor darling has to have regular injections of everything French to keep him going. We've taken up the offer of a house about seventy kilometres south of Beaugency. We shan't be using it all the time, so if any of you want to stay for a few days you're very welcome.'

Later, as his guests were making moves to leave, Adam asked Joe, 'Can you give Freddy a lift home? She walked round.'

'Yes, of course,' Joe replied, and Freddy cringed inwardly, for how could he have refused? When the Tiger pulled up outside Dean Close and Joe followed her to the front door, he asked abruptly, 'How often does Tyson come out from his desk and get behind the camera?'

With the key in the lock, Freddy turned, alert to the sardonic note in his voice. 'Not very often,' she answered levelly. 'He produces more often than he directs. Why?'

'I wonder what the incentive is to take him to France...could it be your presence there?'

'Other than the reason he gave us, I don't know, and what's more, I don't care! It has nothing to do with me.'

'If you say so, Fred,' was Joe's laconic reply and he turned to go.

Really annoyed now, Freddy's arm shot out and she caught hold of him, staying his progress. 'Damn you, Joe, I shouldn't care what you think, but stupidly I do, God knows why! I have never given Patrick any encouragement—how many times do I have to tell you for you to believe me?'

'But you will agree now that I was right about him?'

Freddy struggled with a denial, but honesty won. 'Well, yes, but...'

'I gather confirmation came on the trip north to fetch the Renault?' Joe's voice was dry.

Exasperated, she burst out, 'Yes, you were right! You're not always right, Joe, but this time you were! Satisfied?'

'It's a pity some things become corny, but to hell with it!' He swung her round so what light there was fell on her face. 'When you're fighting mad, Fred, you're very desirable.' And he brought his mouth down on hers, his arms tightening round her.

For some seconds Freddy, constrained against his chest, pushed against him, her hands clenched into fists, feebly battering his shoulders, the rest of her arms imprisoned. When she was released Joe still held her by the elbows and surveyed her ragged

breathing and flushed cheeks with some satisfaction. 'It matters that I believe you, Fred?'

She wrenched her arms free and, goaded, replied, 'Yes, damn you!'

He searched her face, gave a small nod of the
head. 'I believe you,' he said softly and then walked
swiftly back down the path.

Freddy let out a frustrated breath, grinding her
teeth in exasperation before sweeping inside.

Two weeks later she parked the Renault outside
the rehearsal building and slipped inside. She was
dropping in more often than was needed, making
some excuse to warrant the journey. As she had
forecast, Joe was becoming a drug.

She watched him now, talking to the black actor
playing Othello. The actor, Baz, was a large, well
proportioned man, beautiful in face and form, and
with a magnetism that suited the part of the Moor.
By contrast, Nina Welsh made a perfect Desdemona, Othello's wife, frail and beautiful, her
fairness adding to the contrast.

Joe called the fight instructor over and began to
go through some of the moves. Nina, waiting at
the side, had a sulky expression on her face and on
Freddy's entrance had given her a sharp, almost
challenging look. What's the matter with Madam?
wondered Freddy, using the nickname the crew had
bestowed on Nina.

'Good morning, Freddy,' said David.

Freddy returned his smile and murmured, 'Hello,
David, anything to report?'

'One or two things.' He fell silent and watched
with her. To demonstrate what he wanted, Joe had

taken up one of the practice swords and was engaged in a slow motion fight with the instructor, each move exaggerated and perfectly executed.

Joe called for a break and walked over, asking David, 'Have you told her yet?'

'Told me what?' demanded Freddy, looking from one to the other.

David replied, 'No, not yet,' his voice mild.

'Perhaps you could now do so?' suggested Joe smoothly. 'Let's find somewhere private, shall we?' He strode off towards a small storage-room. Exchanging looks, David and Freddy followed.

'The problem is,' David explained, 'that Miss Welsh lost her temper, and wants our assurance that we won't use that clip in the programme.'

Freddy gave a laugh which she choked off when she saw they were serious. 'You've got to be joking!' She turned to Joe, who was leaning against the wall contemplating his shoes. 'Apart from the fact that I don't take kindly to having my programme edited for me, I can hardly see that a tantrum thrown by one of the actors is anything to get paranoid about.'

She swung back to David, who was having difficulty with his mouth. 'Actually, Freddy,' he said gravely, 'this couldn't be termed a tantrum, more a major eruption.'

Joe remained silent.

Freddy bit off an exclamation and ran fingers through her hair. 'We can't make any decisions until we've seen the rushes. Surely Nina understands that? We are, after all, intending to give the flavour of these rehearsals as well as the development, warts and all. You'll have to tell her that. I'm sorry I can't be more explicit.'

Joe gave a nod and opened the door for her to pass. He went straight into rehearsal, ignoring the speculative looks exchanged by the cast and crew. Nina refused to catch their eye and threw herself into her speech, giving an exceedingly good performance.

'I did wonder if you'd let Madam off the hook,' murmured David.

'You didn't expect me to, did you?' retorted Freddy.

'No, but I wouldn't have blamed you. Poor old Corey will have to bear the brunt.'

'I'm sure he's more than capable.'

David chuckled. 'It was a humdinger of a row, Freddy, but you'll be able to see for yourself when we watch the rushes.'

Freddy did see, and although it was not too clear why Nina had lost her temper, whatever it was that had triggered it, all hell had been let loose. Freddy ran the film back and re-ran it, watching Joe intently. She could read nothing from his features to give a clue as to what he had been thinking while it had been going on.

When she switched off the projector and David put on the light, she remarked, 'As you said, some humdinger. I can understand why she doesn't want it broadcast to the nation!' She grinned. 'What a pity we don't feel justified in using it.' She thought for a moment. 'It might be interesting to use that long shot from camera three for a few seconds.'

'I thought as part of the background to the opening credits,' suggested David, and Freddy laughed, shaking her head reprovingly.

'How wicked you are, David!'

'She's a spoilt little madam,' excused David, 'and the long shots are rather good. We'll try it and see what it looks like, shall we?'

Nina came up to Freddy the following day, asking if any decision had been reached.

Freddy said, 'I doubt we'll use it, Nina, and if we do it will only be for a few seconds, just to show the tensions. Nothing you need worry about.'

'I should like to be the judge of that,' Nina replied coldly, and called Joe. He came over, the scenic designer trailing after him with swatches of materials in his hands, their discussion interrupted.

'Joe, Miss Leigh won't give me a definite answer,' Nina told him, slipping her arm through his in a distinctively personal manner. 'I had hoped she'd be able to.'

'I warned you not to expect anything cut and dried, Nina,' Joe said patiently, and Freddy thought it time to have her say.

'I'm afraid I can't be more definite,' she said firmly and would have given a great deal to know what Joe was thinking. Could he be attracted to someone like Nina Welsh, she wondered, beautiful and talented, yet selfish and spoilt? As she watched them return to the rehearsal Freddy decided darkly that artistic tantrums were not confined to just actors. If they didn't watch out she would throw one herself!

She turned to go and saw that David and the crew were grinning, and she realised she had been on camera. She pulled a face at them and left.

# CHAPTER EIGHT

FREDDY fell in love with Beaugency the moment she saw the beautiful bridge over the wide, graceful Loire, its waters bubbling over boulders scattered around the base of the perfectly symmetrical arches.

If the bridge wasn't enough to capture her, there was the town itself, with its grey rough-stone buildings and narrow cobbled streets. Freddy had arrived two days earlier, before everyone else, and most of her work was now done, all of it preparatory, ensuring that the filming would run smoothly. Today she had fixed up a storage-room to house their equipment and had looked over and confirmed accommodation for the crew.

She was lodging in a small boarding house whose windows opened out on to an attractive flower-edged street. It was a delightful June day, and as she leaned out of one of these windows Freddy knew that she was really only marking time until Joe arrived. It was ridiculous but true, and needed to be stated. She felt neither in control over herself or her future. He had managed to invade the physical space inside her head and do treacherous things to her heart and body. She found she was constantly going off in a daydream—even the inner exhilaration she felt when she saw him, the warmth that spread through her, she was beginning to accept as normal.

Freddy glanced at her watch and withdrew from the window. Here she was, mooning over Joe when she should be working. Gradually, over the next couple of hours, the Queen's and Atticus people began to arrive and things began to get hectic as she directed her own team into parking spaces and hotels. The town was wearing a festive air and was thronged with holidaymakers—hopefully, some of them would be making up the audience of *Othello*.

Freddy bumped into Joe, literally, as she was coming out of one of the offices in the château and her heart leaped into her throat as, for a second, they came into contact. They both apologised and Joe swept his eyes over her. Taking in the slight tan she had acquired during the two days, he drawled, 'Been lazing in the sun, Fred?'

His eyes were amused as she opened her mouth indignantly to deny she had been anything but lazy, and then she bit the words back, laughed, and gave him the tip of her tongue as an answer. She went on her way, feeling ridiculously happy to have seen him.

The Atticus team, headed by Patrick, descended, *en masse*, at one of the town's bars, and Freddy answered innumerable questions and the final details were ironed out. Thankfully, despite her daydreaming, everything seemed to have been dealt with satisfactorily.

The following morning the courtyard of the château was a hive of industry. Freddy was sitting in a sunny corner, a hat pulled down to shade her face, watching what was going on. Liz slipped into the seat next to her and the two girls smiled a greeting. Joe was standing in the middle of the courtyard, frowning down at the cobbles, obviously puzzling how to overcome a problem.

'I don't envy Joe,' remarked Liz quietly, 'he has a difficult job without much time to do it in.' She glanced thoughtfully from Freddy's face to Joe, who was now getting things moving again, the problem resolved.

'He'll do it,' Freddy claimed confidently. 'Is Adam with you?'

'He's in the château, organising where we can store our wardrobe. If it rains it will be awfully difficult getting the costumes dry, they're all so thick and cumbersome.'

Freddy turned her face to the blue sky. She was wearing a thin, strappy top, cut low back and front in pale yellow, with a floral full skirt. Her legs were bare and she had sandals on her feet. Her hair, for coolness, she had twisted up under the hat. 'I don't think it will rain,' she said, 'the weather seems very settled.'

They fell silent again, watching the play. It was the scene where Othello, in a fit of jealous madness, smothers Desdemona, and it ran without Joe stopping the action.

When Nina fell lifeless on to the mound of cushions heaped on a dais, Liz said softly, frowning a little, 'They're good, aren't they?' She waited for Freddy's nod of agreement and went on, 'I wish I liked Nina better.'

Liz so rarely said anything critical of anyone that Freddy turned a surprised face her way. Liz shrugged. 'Success can come too early for some

people, and I'm afraid Nina's become big-headed.
She's pretty and talented, but she can be a real pain.
However, she's off to make a film in Spain when
*Othello* finishes.' Liz's eyes were guileless as she
gazed at Freddy, although her brain was ticking over
like mad, an idea growing.

'Really? I didn't know that.' Freddy became lost
in thought, her eyes following Joe. He was pointing
directions to his stage manager for the drapes to be
moved. When it was done to his satisfaction he
crossed to one of the pillars that made up the colonnade and leaned against it, hands in pockets, chin
low as he watched the sword fight now in progress.

His arms and legs were bare and tanned and he
was wearing a much washed T-shirt and cut-off
jeans, with canvas shoes on his feet and a battered
denim hat on his head, for the courtyard was a sun-
trap.

Freddy sighed without knowing she did so, and
Liz chewed her bottom lip, interest quickening as
she twigged who had caused the sigh. She decided
to do some testing, and said, 'Adam told me about
Nina's little outburst.'

'Not so little,' observed Freddy with a grin. Joe
had turned and was looking their way. Her pulse
quickened. Was he coming over to speak? No. He
swung away and began to talk to the carpenter. 'I
hope Adam wasn't too cross that I couldn't say
anything definite about cutting it,' she added
anxiously.

'Quite the reverse. He knew you couldn't. Joe
was furious you even had to be asked, but he
thought it politic to keep Nina happy.'

'Joe did?' The flecks of green in Freddy's eyes seemed to lighten as she turned to Liz.

'Uh-huh—he made a few cryptic remarks to Adam about it.'

Freddy hid her delight and her spirits lifted. Joe had understood and approved. Well, of course he had! He was, after all, a professional, like herself. Why on earth should she have supposed otherwise?

'Have you enjoyed doing the Queen's programme?' asked Liz idly, and Freddy smiled and said warmly that she had. 'Adam was most impressed by the bit he's seen, the David Herrick bits, of course. He's also impressed by the way you've handled things, Freddy, which I think is nice to know. He was glad he listened to Joe.'

'How do you mean?'

Liz shrugged. 'When Patrick said they were interested, Joe told Adam to ask for you specifically. Said you were good. And now you've proved it,' and she beamed her congratulations. 'I'm glad you're coming to St Julien,' she went on. 'We shall be going to Paris on the Thursday, so you can have the place to yourself from then. Come on the Wednesday, as planned, and we can show you round locally. Patrick and Dinah are going to Italy, I understand.'

Freddy nodded. She had heard the news with some relief. She had feared they would be at St Julien too, but now she could look forward to those few days without any reservations.

'Do you think you'll be lonely at St Julien all by yourself, Freddy?' Liz asked with amazing innocence. 'How about me asking Joe to join you there?'

'Don't you dare!' Freddy swung round, horror showing on her face, a wave of red flooding throat and cheeks as she met Liz's look.

Liz said softly, 'So you do love him still.'

'Oh, Lizzie, you are a wretch!' Freddy groaned, mortified, and pulled the brim of her linen sunhat down over her face.

'Adam told me that you and Joe knew each other from some years ago, and something Joe said once made me think you were not just casual friends. I promise I won't give you away, Freddy, and you don't have to tell me if you don't want to, but what the dickens are you doing, mooning over the man and doing nothing about it?'

Freddy lifted her head and pulled a face. 'Oh, Liz, I was so mixed up when he came to Queensbridge, so frightened of falling in love with him all over again, but I thought I could cope, and it's all a mess! I've tried to keep out of his way and everything's conspired to make me do just the opposite! Lizzie, I can't understand him. He's been sweet and kind and he's lovely with Meggie, she adores him, and then he'll be perfectly beastly and practically accuses me of having an affair with Patrick. Oh, he made me so mad! And it didn't stop me falling in love with him, and if you say one word to him about how I feel, Lizzie, I'll...I'll...just die!' The final words came out in a deep groan.

Liz grinned. 'Not a word shall pass my lips.' She stared across at Joe. 'He can be a closed book when he wants, but I've caught Joe looking at you a few times in unguarded moments, and I could hardly call his expression indifferent. Is whatever's keeping you apart insoluble?'

Freddy pushed the brim of her hat up with one finger and blew out a breath, the heat in her cheeks fading slightly. 'I don't know. I think he's given me up.' She laughed low in her throat, ruefully. 'Ironic, isn't it? I tell him to leave me alone and when he does I can't bear it!'

'Well, if Nina is one of your worries, I think you can forget her. She isn't Joe's type.' Liz tilted her head at her friend and went on, 'Why don't you sit down and just talk to him? So often we're saying one thing and meaning something completely different. Try words of one syllable for a change. And now I must go. I can see Adam waiting for me.' She covered Freddy's hand with her own for a second; the two women exchanged smiles, and Liz left.

Freddy made her way back to the *pension* not long after. More than anything she wanted to talk to Joe, but now wasn't the time. She had already decided she would tell him how she felt, that she was prepared to live with him if he still wanted her. And if he did, she wouldn't think about the future, but would take what happiness she and Megan could find while it was offered them. What she would do if he turned her down she didn't allow herself to contemplate.

The play opened to a good house. The evening was warm and dry, and the audience surprised and a little flattered to learn that they were being filmed.

Dinah, seated next to Freddy, murmured, 'It's going well. Patrick should be getting some good footage.'

Freddy nodded. Try as she might she couldn't feel totally relaxed in Dinah's company. She never had been able to and it was even more difficult since Patrick had declared himself, although her conscience was clear. She felt a stirring of pity for the Tysons. Perhaps there had been a time when each might have sought happiness with someone else, but Atticus seemed to have tied them together too securely.

Sitting on the other side of Freddy was Joe. He was so close that his arm was touching hers. She could have found a way of moving so that it didn't, but she stayed where she was, and suddenly realised that if she could move so could Joe. That meant something, surely? She tried to concentrate on the play, but the warmth of his bare flesh overtook everything else. Yet what she felt for him wasn't merely physical, it was much more than that. She loved him for his whole self—his intellect and intelligence, his sense of humour and his compassion.

The applause at the end of *Othello* was encouraging. The audience was mostly French, with a scattering of Germans, Dutch and English. As Shakespeare was so famous and English taught in most European countries, the fact that the text was in that language had not put people off from coming. As the crowd dispersed, the Queen's and Atticus people began to stand around in groups, discussing the performance.

Freddy was with a Frenchman, one of the Festival organisers. Luckily he spoke good English, and Freddy was enjoying talking to him and his wife. Adam had ordered a buffet and wine to be served after the show, and had invited some of the French people who had been closely involved to join them.

Patrick and Dinah wandered over and Patrick said quietly to Freddy, 'Well done! Everything was beautifully planned, as is usual when you're the producer.' He made as if to say more, but Dinah asked him a question and he gave Freddy a smile, and a nod of approval, before turning to answer his wife.

Slightly on the outside of the group, Freddy lifted her eyes and found herself staring across the courtyard straight at Joe. Like her, he had a glass of wine in his hand, and, sharply reminiscent of their meeting at the Atticus party, he lifted the glass to her in salute. This time she returned the gesture and they both drank, their eyes still upon each other.

How long ago the Atticus party seemed! Yet, in another way, that September evening, nine months ago, could have been yesterday.

Joe began to walk slowly towards her and she went to meet him. When they were a hand reach away they stopped.

Freddy said, 'Congratulations, Joe.'

He inclined his head and drawled, 'You needn't spare my blushes if you want to criticise, Fred. I have a tiny feeling that you have reservations.'

Freddy hid her surprise. How on earth had he guessed? 'I've enjoyed watching the play grow,' she admitted, 'and it's one of the best *Othello*s I've seen, but I can't like the play.'

Joe's brows rose quizzically. 'Why not?'

Actors were spilling out from the colonnade, and laughter and conversation was rising in the late evening air. Freddy was in a sleeveless dress and Joe in a short-sleeved shirt, yet it was still warm. No one came to disturb them. They were isolated in the middle of the courtyard and Freddy was hardly aware of what was going on around her, only of Joe.

'Because I can't bear jealousy in any form,' she replied slowly. 'It's such a degrading emotion and Shakespeare has come to the final extremes in *Othello*. It frightens me, in myself and in others.'

Joe said softly, 'Well, well, I never thought I'd hear Frederica Leigh admit to being frightened.'

'That's silly, everyone's frightened of something.'

'I thought you were invincible, Fred, and needed no one. That's the act you put about, isn't it?' His tone was light, yet his eyes searched her face intently.

Freddy had trouble meeting those eyes. Faint colour touched her cheeks and she looked down at her sandalled foot, smoothing her toe across the cobbles.

'Only because I'm scared of making a fool of myself,' she replied, giving a rueful smile.

'And do you ever succumb to this dangerous emotion, jealousy, Frederica?'

She lifted her head at this, and green eyes locked with brown.

'Yes, of course I do. Doesn't everyone?' She paused and her heartbeat quickened as she added, 'I understand Nina is going to Spain.'

Joe's lashes lifted slightly and his face stilled. 'Do you find that interesting?'

'I wondered if she would have you there, to show her the ropes.' There, it was out, and not so difficult after all.

Joe's lashes came down again and he drawled, 'I have no desire to go anywhere with Nina. I have other plans.'

A warmth was creeping through her. 'Oh?'

'I'm building a house. In Queensbridge.'

'Oh!' Really, she was beginning to look like a fish, mouthing 'oh' all the time!

Joe might have been going to say more, but his name was called. 'We'll talk about this later, shall we?' he suggested, a tiny smile creasing the side of his mouth, and then he was drawn into a group of Beaugency dignitaries who were being entertained by Liz and Adam.

In bed that night Freddy savoured every look, every word, alternating between despair that she was seeing too much into what was said, and incredible joy that she might be able to put things right between them. She wouldn't speculate on the future, the future could take care of itself. She would take each day as it came.

Freddy left Beaugency, driving south, taking her time and enjoying the countryside. She reached St Julien and the Carlyons' white house with its shuttered windows in the early evening. Inside it was cool, the thick stone walls and flagged floors keeping out the heat, and was beautiful in an austere way. She chose a bedroom overlooking the meadows and the river, and opened the window to get a better view. A deep purple clematis clung to the wall outside and she breathed in the sweet evening air and thought about Joe. He had gone to Paris the day before, very early, so that she had not spoken to him and was still in no man's land, yet this did not worry her. On her return to Queensbridge she would tell him she loved him. What happened then was up to him.

She awoke the next morning to find brilliant sunshine streaming through the window, and after breakfasting on coffee and croissants by the side of the river she found the bicycle that Liz had said was in the shed and set off with lunch bought from the village shop-post office. Wearing shorts and a sun top, and with a cotton scarf tied round her head, she was soon bowling along the lanes in search of a local château.

One particular village was her aim and she reached it just on midday. As was usual at this time the village was deserted, and Freddy could find no one to ask if she could take a look at the château, but the gate in the huge stone wall that encircled the gardens was unlocked. She leaned the cycle against the wall, which was at least fourteen feet high, and the door yielded to her touch. She passed through, closing it behind her.

It was as though she had stepped into one of the fairy-tales out of Megan's book. An enchanted place! The air was still and the quiet was broken only by birdsong. Everything in the grounds was overgrown and neglected, and yet this only added to its charm. The château was small, rounded and turreted, encircled by a still, dark green moat over which there was a tiny bridge leading to a tall wooden door. This, as were the shutters on the windows, was firmly shut.

Freddy walked like a sleeping person, drifting through long grass in the orchard, the trees misshapen and old, delighting in the butterflies flitting to and fro and the fish, dark streaks, darting beneath the algae lying on the surface of the water.

It was too hot to stay in the sun for long. Freddy retraced her steps, intending to fetch her lunch and sit under the trees. Before she reached the door in the wall, however, her attention was caught by a collection of brasses hanging on the outside of a dilapidated stable. She studied them with interest and stepped in at the open door. Inside, piled high, was hay and straw. She closed her eyes and conjured up a vision of the château in its heyday, with horses hooves sounding on the cobbles of the yard, grooms running to obey orders, a dog barking...

A noise outside made her jump. Had it been the door banging shut in the wall? She listened intently, suddenly unsure of her position here. Footsteps sounded on the cobbles and a shadow passed by the dusty, cobwebbed window. A man, by size and shape.

A farmer? Another tourist? Whoever it was, she was here, on her own, which wasn't particularly clever.

This is silly, she told herself sternly, feeling her heart thumping with nerves. You're allowing your imagination to run away with you. She frowned, listening hard. Had he, whoever he was, gone on to the château? Suddenly, just as she was deciding to make her escape, she heard a monotonous under-the-breath whistling and realised that there must be another door into the stables further down and that the whistling was coming nearer.

Without thinking, Freddy picked up a broom handle lying handy, and stepped back behind a large wooden down-beam against which straw was piled. Then, at the last minute, she wondered what on earth she was doing, and decided to make a dash for it. She leaped for the opening, flinging away the broom handle as she went. A strangled yelp sounded from behind, followed by a suppressed oath.

Ten strides and she was out of the stables and lunging at the door in the wall, another two and she was through, gasping for breath, and then she was staring, wide-eyed, at the bright red Tiger parked alongside her cycle.

# CHAPTER NINE

FREDDY turned and marched back into the stables. Where was the wretch? she raged inwardly, and glanced round wildly. A movement on one of the bales of straw attracted her attention and she saw it was Joe, lying flat on his back, arms outstretched. Her mouth went dry with apprehension and she rushed forward, dropping to her knees.

'Joe!' she cried, and shook him. 'Joe, if you're play-acting, I'll murder you!'

A pained voice replied, 'If this headache is acting, then it's damned realistic.' His eyes opened and his arms came up and she was rolled over on to the straw.

'You brute!' Relief turned to indignation. 'How could you frighten the life out of me that way! Creeping up like that! If you're not hurt you jolly well should be!' Her fists flailed his shoulders.

Joe caught them and pinned them down. 'Dear girl, I had no idea you would be frightened. I didn't even know you were in here, I thought you'd be in the château...'

'You can't go in the château!'

'...and the brasses caught my attention and I thought I'd take a look before going to find you. What on earth were you doing, skulking in here, brandishing a blunt instrument?'

'I was looking at the brasses, you idiot!' howled Freddy. 'Let me up, Joe, damn you,' and she strugged ineffectually to free herself.

'I think I deserve a bit of sympathy,' Joe said reproachfully. 'After all, being knocked out by a broom handle is no fun.'

Freddy stopped struggling and now saw a rapidly discolouring bump on his forehead, from which ran a trickle of blood.

Remorse swept over her, but she wasn't ready to capitulate so soon. 'It didn't knock you out,' she accused.

'Poetic licence,' explained Joe, pained.

'You were playing on my sympathy and ... and scaring me out of my wits!'

The laughter died in his face and he said quietly, 'I'm sorry, Frederica, that was the last thing I intended.'

'Oh, really?' The sarcasm was half-hearted. The look on his face was making breathing difficult. 'And just what is it that brings you here?' She waited for him to speak, feeling his heart pounding against her breast. His brows rose quizzically and his mouth turned downwards, so Joseph-like, that she wanted to touch his lips with her fingertips and smooth them out, take away their cynical curves.

'I wanted to find you,' Joe said, 'and do this.' And his head came down, his eyes still holding hers, and he rested his mouth on her lips, gently, and sweet pleasure rushed through her. When he raised his head finally, his voice was husky. 'You can box my ears now, if you like,' he told her, releasing her

wrists. When she made no move to do as he suggested, he kissed her again.

This time Freddy gave in to something she had
been promising herself for a long time. Her hands
came up, and her fingers spread themselves in the
hair at the nape of his neck and she was kissing
him back, abandoning all pretence, all indif-
ference, desire erupting like a volcano.

In the space between the kisses, Joe said roughly,
'This is it, Fred, now or never. I can't concentrate
on anything any more, I keep seeing your beautiful
green eyes——' and here he kissed them, one at a
time '—and your darling of a mouth——' and this,
too, received like treatment '—and it's been hell
keeping my hands off you, either to shake some
sense into your cuckoo head or make love to you,
or both!'

'What a brute,' breathed Freddy, laughter in her
voice.

'I want you to give us a chance, Frederica. It's
crazy not to.'

'Yes, please, Joe.'

'We'll take it a day at a time, but you owe it to
us both to give it a try...' He stilled. 'What did
you say?' he demanded.

'I said, yes, please, Joe. I've stopped running,
and there's a lethal piece of straw sticking into my
rear end.'

There was silence while Joe searched her face.
'Then we shall have to do something about it,' he
drawled, his eyes gleaming with elation. He rolled
over so that Freddy was now lying on him and he

smoothed his hands all over her, brushing away the bits of straw, being practical at first and then indulging in the feel of the curve of her back, and the roundness of her rump. 'Better?' he asked.

Freddy murmured languidly, 'Much better.' She touched his face, running her fingers along his jaw, outlining his ear, and he caught the hand, and turned the palm to his mouth to kiss it.

'I'm getting too old for playing games in the hay,' he groaned, 'so we'll find somewhere more satisfactory, mm?'

'Is that a promise?' asked Freddy, allowing him to haul her to her feet. 'You look like the strawman from Oz,' she told him, laughing, and began to pick the straw out of his hair. Her gaze lingered on the cut on his forehead. 'Poor Joe, does it hurt?' she asked anxiously.

'Like hell,' he replied cheerfully. He took her hand and led her out of the stable and they stood blinking in the bright sunlight. 'I've brought lunch

'So have I,' broke in Freddy.

'Shall we sit in the orchard?' he asked. 'I'm sure no one will mind, and you can tell me how much you love me.'

'Is that an order?' she teased gently.

Joe lifted her hand and held it against his face, his eyes darkening with feeling. 'There are some words of a song I can't get out of my head. Something like freedom's just another word for nothing left to lose.' He smiled. 'People have some funny ideas about freedom, Frederica, and some day I'll tell you what I think it means. Right now I'm parched and there's some wine on ice in the Tiger. Let's fetch it.'

'Did Lizzie say anything to you, Joe?' Freddy lay back on his chest, eating a succulent yellow plum, looking up through the trees at the blue sky.

'What could Liz have told me?' questioned Joe, gently winding a strand of her hair round his finger.

'Well, she guessed how I felt about you,' murmured Freddy.

'And how could that be described?' A brow rose quizzically.

She gave a muted laugh deep in her throat. 'Furiously angry, wonderfully happy, dizzy with longing, miserable with jealousy, acting my head off so that you shouldn't guess, wanting to give in, yet fearful of you leaving me...'

'I'll not leave you,' Joe said firmly and sealed the promise with a kiss. Some very satisfying minutes later, he went on, 'Actually, it's Adam we have to thank.'

'Adam?' Surprise coloured Freddy's voice. 'Good gracious! Why?' And she twisted round to look at him.

'It was through Adam that I came to Queensbridge in the first place,' explained Joe. 'We met up in London and talk came round to Atticus. I mentioned that I knew someone who worked for that company and asked Adam if he knew you. If I'd asked Liz no doubt she would have mentioned Megan, but Adam merely told me that he understood you were divorced.'

'But you pretended you didn't know,' Freddy protested.

'Yes, well, it wouldn't have done to lay all my cards on the table at once,' teased Joe, enfolding her hand in his and bringing it to his lips. 'Patrick Tyson had been on at me for some time to let Atticus do an adaption of *Wandering Man*. I suddenly decided to take him up on the offer.'

'So you came looking for me!' The idea took some getting used to.

'It's not often a man gets to having a second chance of winning the woman he stupidly lost in the first place. And when we finally meet, what do I find? A Frederica looking more beautiful than ever, cool and poised and very able to do without me.'

'Not true,' declared Freddy lovingly. 'When I saw you I felt as though I'd been hit on the head by a brick dropped from a great height. I was devastated by all the old longings.'

Joe gave a short laugh. 'It didn't look that way to me. Each time I thought we were making some headway, you kept retreating.'

Freddy rolled over, wound her arms round his neck and nuzzled him, laughing softly. 'I was scared stiff you'd make me fall in love with you all over again,' she admitted ruefully. 'I wanted to run a mile and yet be with you. Awfully uncomfortable. It's what is called being torn apart,' she added gravely.

'I know the feeling,' he drawled. 'I didn't mind you running—so long as you stopped eventually. I just didn't want you to run into the arms of Patrick Tyson!'

Freddy groaned. 'And what,' she demanded severely, 'was I supposed to do about Nina Welsh?'

Joe grinned. 'How could you think there was anything between Nina and myself?'

She poked him in the ribs with a stern finger. 'You meant me to think there was, you wretch!' She lay back on the grass and sighed deeply with satisfaction. 'Isn't it just perfect, this place? Joe, how did you know I'd be here?'

'I knew from the Carlyons that you were going to St Julien, and the woman in the village shop told me you had asked about the way to the château— so here I am, bloody but unbowed.' He half sat up and studied her face. 'You knew I'd come, Fred,' he chided gently, and his fingers traced the line of her jaw.

'Yes, I knew—well, hoped, but I thought I'd have to wait until I returned home.' Freddy paused. 'Joe, you have thought about Megan, haven't you? I mean, she's part of my life, and whatever happens in the future . . .'

'She will be part of it,' finished Joe, putting a finger on her lips to stop the words. 'Meggie and I understand each other perfectly, Fred, darling, and we both love you very much.'

'Meggie and I love you, too,' confided Freddy. She smiled sleepily, the sun warm on her face. 'This might, of course, turn out to be a dream,' she murmured. 'Lovely, lovely dream.'

Her eyelids closed, she sighed deeply and drifted
into sleep. When she woke she couldn't remember
where she was for a moment, and then she saw Joe
lying there beside her, breathing steadily, eyes
closed. Happiness coursed its way through her. She
lovingly, hungrily feasted her eyes on him as he lay
oblivious, one arm folded under his head, the other
lying across his chest. He was wearing a cream
cotton shirt, unbuttoned at the neck, with light
khaki trousers, and she wondered if he would wake
up if she kissed the hollow just below his Adam's
apple. It was such a tempting hollow, a lovely
speckled brown colour, touched with moisture. His
lashes, dark and thick, fanned his cheeks, his mouth
was soft and relaxed and there were tiny beads of
moisture on his upper lip, too.

'If you look at me like that, you'll get eaten,'
murmured Joe, his lips barely moving, his eyes still
closed.

'What a sneaky thing to do, pretending to be
asleep,' remonstrated Freddy softly. She sat up and
spread an arm either side of his chest, palms flat
on the ground. 'If anyone is going to be doing the
eating, it's me.' She bent and gently placed her
mouth in the hollow.

Joe groaned a sigh. Freddy touched her lips to
all parts of his face, ignoring his mouth, teasing
him with the tip of her tongue, finally hovering over
his mouth, keeping her eyes firmly on their outline,
knowing that his lashes were lifted and his eyes were
no longer sleepy. She lowered herself and blew
softly on to his face, still not catching his eyes, and

then touched his lips with the tantalising tip of her tongue.

Joe's hands came up and caught her hair, holding her captive. His eyes were gleaming and he sat up, demanding, 'What the devil are you trying to do to me, woman, make me forget where we are?' He rolled over, sprang to his feet and softly threatened, 'I'll remember all that later and pay you back with interest.' He held out his hands and hauled her, flushed and smiling, to her feet.

They collected their things together and walked slowly through the orchard.

'I feel as though we're in a dream,' murmured Freddy, glancing back at the château, which was as deserted-looking as ever. The heat haze hung over the roof and the trees and it was almost as if time stood still, that it made no impression on this place.

Joe opened the door in the wall and they passed through.

Freddy said laughingly, 'I think you drive the right car, Joe. Innocuous-looking when it's sleeping, dangerous when it's moving, just like a tiger with its prey.'

Joe grinned. 'Prey usually means a helpless victim. I hardly think the term applies to you, girl-dear!' He grimaced and covered his bruised forehead with his palm, pretending pain. He dumped the cycle in the back of the Tiger, easy to do with the soft cover off, and when everything was stowed away they set off back to St Julien.

The white house was cool and silent.

'This time,' Joe said softly, 'we know why we're doing this, don't we?' He gently drew away the sun top from her shoulders and ran his lips slowly along their curve, his hands drifting down to clasp her waist. 'In Yorkshire, I rather felt it was a form of exorcism.'

Freddy arched her back, gazing into his eyes which were dark and intense. She laughed low in her throat, remembering. 'If it was,' she told him breathlessly, 'it didn't work.' She undid the buttons on his shirt and spread her palms across his chest, lingering over his heart, revelling in the strong beat. Joe lifted her on to the bed and began to re-enact her lovemaking of the afternoon, beginning with her face and then trailing a random path all over her body.

Freddy gasped with pleasure as the sneaking tip of his tongue teased and thrilled. 'I give in, Joe, please... oh!'

She dug her fingers in his hair and they fought, laughing a little, the laughter dying, and there was no past, only the present, and everything was wonderful, triumphant and earth-shattering.

A rapping at the front door roused them. Joe looked at Freddy with raised brows, left the bed and threw on some clothes. Freddy waited for him to return, wondering what it was.

'Get dressed, Fred, a message has come through for you to ring home,' Joe said, coming in quickly. 'No, don't panic. Your parents were quite firm that you were not to worry.'

While he was speaking Freddy was dressing in rapid haste. 'It's Meggie. It must be. God, what's happened to her?'

'Hey, calm down. Let's not cross our bridges. We can use the phone at the shop.'

'How did they find the number?' asked Freddy, as they hurried across the village square. It was nearly dusk, but the men were still playing boule. There was a chorus of *'Bonsoir, monsieur, madame,'* as they circled the game, and Joe replied for them both, with Freddy managing a slightly distracted smile.

'I suppose your parents got in touch with the people at Beaugency,' Joe said, pushing open the shop door. 'Beaugency would have put them on to Adam and Liz in Paris.'

Freddy waited in a fever of anxiety while Joe made the connection to England.

'Mrs Leigh? Joseph Corey here. I understand you want to speak to Frederica. She's here now.'

Joe handed the phone to Freddy, who said quickly, 'Mother, what's wrong?'

'Darling, I hope you weren't too upset by my message?' Catherine's voice was calm. 'Do you think you can telephone home tomorrow and speak to Meggie? She had an accident and she's missing you rather.'

'What kind of accident?' demanded Freddy, her heart thumping.

'Nothing very dreadful, but not very pleasant, either. She was knocked down by two boys on bicycles, riding on the pavement, which of course they shouldn't have been doing. They were racing each other and came round the corner, and both ran right into her. She's full of cuts and bruises, but nothing's broken. It shook her up, naturally, and because she hit her head we took her to the hospital, but the X-ray didn't show anything and they didn't want to keep her in. The two boys ought to have known better, but they're very sorry, and their parents have been round.'

'So I should think! Wretched boys—why couldn't they look where they were going?' exclaimed Freddy angrily. 'You're sure Megan's OK, Mother? You're not keeping anything from me, are you? I'd rather know.'

'Darling, everything is just as I've said,' soothed Catherine.

'Poor Meg! I shall come home tomorrow—tell her, will you?'

'We'll both be home tomorrow,' said Joe, leaning across and speaking into the telephone while he held Freddy with a strong protective arm.

There was a smile in Catherine's voice. 'I'm so glad Joseph is with you, Freddy. I was worried that you might be on your own.' There was a pause before she added delicately, 'Is everything well between you and Joseph, darling?'

'Everything's wonderful,' replied her daughter.

They set off for home early the next morning, Joe driving the Tiger, Freddy the Renault. Freddy had accepted Megan's accident for what it was, one of those happenings that could have been worse. Each time she caught sight of the red sports car in her mirror a rush of happiness rippled through her, and she thought how lucky she and Megan were, to have Joe become part of their family.

Arriving at Dean Close a little travel-weary, Megan did look rather a mess and cried when she saw them, but the tears were soon dried when Joe set out to make her laugh, and she was allowed to stay up a little longer than usual that evening.

No questions were asked by Catherine and Edmund Leigh before they set off for their own home in Boston, although privately they were over-joyed at the happiness glowing from their daughter.

Joe's quiet, 'Don't worry about them,' and his quick grin, followed by, 'She's finally stopped running,' settled their surmising of the future.

Judith was not so reticent. She was most verbal. 'I just wish I'd taken on a bet with you,' she told Freddy, when Joe finally left. '"I'm not getting married again! I'm off marriage",' she mimicked.

Freddy burst out laughing and threw an accurate cushion at her friend, protesting, 'He hasn't asked me to marry him, Judith!'

'He will,' prophesied Judith smugly.

A week later, following instructions from Joe, Freddy glanced at her watch and hurried her steps through the shopping precinct, her hand clutching Megan's tightly, the little girl having to run at her side to keep up. Even for a Saturday, Queensbridge was crowded and the traffic was almost crawling to a standstill.

'Will Joseph be there, Mummy?' Megan asked, panting with the exertion.

'He said he would be,' replied Freddy, wondering what Joe was up to. He had rung her that morning, offering to pick her up in town, although where he had told her to meet him—outside the Queen's Theatre—was hardly a convenient picking-up point.

'There he is,' shouted Megan, letting go her mother's hand and running on ahead. Freddy saw the gleaming red paintwork of the Tiger first, with Houdini sitting majestically on the back seat. Then she saw Joe, leaning against the wing, talking to a traffic warden, a buxom lady, who was trying to look severe and not succeeding.

As Freddy and Megan neared they could hear Joe saying, 'Yes, I know it's a double yellow line, but surely a flat tyre constitutes an emergency?'

'And you say that your young lady is on her way?' questioned the warden.

'Two of them, actually.' Joe had seen them, but made no move to declare the fact. Freddy held Megan back, eyeing him suspiciously.

'And it's her turn to do the mechanical duties?' The warden announced that as if repeating a quote, her voice doubtful.

'Quite correct,' Joe drawled. 'This week the roster runs that I do the cooking. I have a goose in the oven at the moment—you've heard the expression to cook one's own goose? I'm cooking mine.'

Freddy spluttered a laugh, and moved forward, saying, 'Hello, darling, is there something wrong?'

Joe's smile broke out like the sun. 'Here she is. Darling! I've got a flat tyre!'

'Oh dear, never mind. Don't you worry about it. We'll soon have that changed, won't we, Meggie?'

Megan nodded and smiled radiantly at Joe. She still looked as though she had been in the wars, but the bruises and scratches were fading rapidly.

Joe scooped her into his arms, saying, 'Hello, princess.'

'Are you really going to change the wheel?' asked the warden, looking dubiously at Freddy's pale lemon dress.

'It looks like it,' she replied cheerfully.

'There's a pair of overalls in the boot,' Joe informed her kindly. Two more pedestrians slowed their steps, curiosity getting the better of them. Inside the boot was the spare tyre, the jack, a box of tools and the promised pair of overalls, pristine white. Joe glanced at his watch. 'I need to get back in an hour to baste the bird,' he told Freddy worriedly. 'Do you think we'll make it?'

A bus pulled up, waiting for traffic to pass the other way before overtaking the Tiger. The passengers gawped as it began to inch by.

'So we have goose tonight, have we?' Freddy asked, struggling into the overalls, and one of the pedestrians remarked to her neighbour, 'Goose is awful rich—repeats something wicked.' Freddy caught Joe's eye and saw he was having to hide his amusement.

'We do if you get a move on,' he said.

Freddy glared at him. He would pay dearly for this later, but right now she would play his game for him.

'You've got her well trained, mate,' joked the bus driver, poking his head out of the cab window.

'She's very independent,' drawled Joe. 'I'm just putting her through her paces before I ask her to marry me.'

The spectators grinned and chuckled and one woman said, 'Go to it, girl! Show the men we're as good as they are.'

'He's cooking the dinner tonight,' the warden called out to the bus driver, feeling she ought to be more in control of the situation, but too intrigued and charmed to interfere.

A car hooted behind the bus indignantly and the driver shouted, 'Good luck, lady,' withdrew his head and drove on.

By now Freddy had the wheel trim off and was jacking the car up from behind the rear bumper. Joe had offered this piece of information, thank goodness, as different cars had different locations for fixing the jack.

'What's the trouble?' A policeman strolled up and was assessing the situation.

'No trouble, officer,' assured Joe. 'We won't be long now.'

The policeman looked from Freddy to Joe and grinned. He stepped on to the roadway and began to direct traffic round the Tiger, glancing now and again to see how Freddy was doing.

She was, in fact, going redder and redder in the face with the exertion of removing the five nuts from the wheel. Joe strolled round to the tool-box in the boot and took out a long-handled brace which he handed silently to her. Puffing slightly, she straightened for a moment, glanced at his deadpan face and then went back to work. The nuts began to give as she was able to apply more pressure, and before long she placed them, one by one, safely in line along the kerb. Now for the spare wheel out of the boot. This, too, was a struggle, but she gritted her teeth and heaved, aware of encouraging words from the rapidly growing crowd of spectators.

'I hope the dinner tonight is going to be good,' she said, breathing heavily as she rolled the spare wheel round to the kerb.

'It will be,' promised Joe airily. 'There's goose, of course, with all the trimmings, a choice of four veggies, and I thought pavlova or fresh fruit salad for afters.'

'Blimey,' said a male voice from the back, 'can I come?'

'Need any help, love?' asked a passing builder's labourer.

'Everything's fine, thanks,' muttered Freddy, adding under her breath, 'at the minute!' She was wrestling with the wheel on the car. At last, after a huge heave, it came off, dropped to the road with a thud and she struggled with it into the boot. It took some effort and she leaned against the wing, catching her breath.

The next part, she knew from experience, was tricky. She stood up and brushed the hair from her face, leaving a black oil mark across her forehead. She looked challengingly at Joe, who was still holding Megan, her arms clutched round his neck, and he smiled that treacherous smile of his. She found she was grinning back idiotically.

There were five holes in the centre of the new wheel to be fitted on to the five studs on the hub of the car. Freddy manoeuvred the wheel until it was opposite the hub and aligned holes to studs.

'Need help?' quizzed Joe.

'Keep your hands off,' threatened Freddy. '*If* I do, then I'll ask for it.'

'You've picked a busy time of the day to have a puncture,' the policeman remarked, and Joe replied smoothly, 'Punctures have no respect for time, place or person.'

'You can say that again,' muttered Freddy, heaving the wheel up and on, triumphantly levering it into place. There were cries of encouragement, a few handclaps. She fitted the nuts, one by one, starting at the top, and tightening them with a brace, then lowered the jack. Panting, she looked across the car at Joe, waited until she had regained her breath and then held out the brace.

'Now you can apply that extra amount of brute strength that I admit I haven't got and make sure the nuts are tightened adequately.'

He put Megan down and did as she asked, making no comment. When he was done she slotted back the wheel trim, gave it a smart kick with the heel of her shoe and felt it snap on. She put the tools back in the boot and dropped the lid down with a decisive bang.

One elderly gentleman leaned over and patted her shoulder, murmuring, 'Well done, m'dear, well done,' before walking on.

A woman joked, 'His cooking had better be as good, love,' causing much laughter. Gradually they all drifted away.

The traffic warden strolled back and said, 'Right, you two, be off with you, and choose a less busy place next time to do your courting.' She wagged a finger at Joe and then turned to Freddy, asking, 'Are you going to accept him?'

'I think I might,' replied Freddy, looking at Joe and smiling a little.

Joe leaned into the back of the Tiger and produced a bunch of roses which he now presented with a flourish to the warden.

Face bright red, laughing, she clutched them to her and observed to Freddy, 'My, he's a dangerous fellow!' and, still shaking her head, she walked on.

'Your flowers, Fred,' Joe said comically. 'Hope you don't mind. I'll buy you some more.'

Freddy burst into laughter, she just couldn't hold it in any longer. She wiped her hands down the by now not-so-pristine overalls and stripped them off, tossing them on to the floor in the back of the car. Joe lifted Megan into the back seat, and strapped her in. Then he got out a clean handkerchief, said, 'You've passed full marks,' and wiped the black smudge from her forehead. He opened the passenger door with a grand air and ushered Freddy in. The policeman halted the oncoming traffic to let them move off, grinning as they passed him.

'Are you going to marry me, Frederica?' asked Joe.

'I didn't think you were the marrying kind,' she teased.

'I'm not, if I can't have you.'

'I can be bridesmaid,' piped up Megan from the back, 'and Joseph will be with us all the time!'

'You'd better marry me,' Joe advised, eyes amused. 'The child and the dog will make your life a misery if you don't.'

Freddy glanced over her shoulder. Houdini's black squashed-up muzzle and soulful brown eyes and Megan's anxious little pixie face were both fixed on her intently. She gave Megan a wink and turned to Joe.

His brows rose questioningly as he flicked her a wicked side glance. 'So, will you marry me, Fred?'

Freddy grinned. 'I'll let you know when I've tasted the goose,' she said.

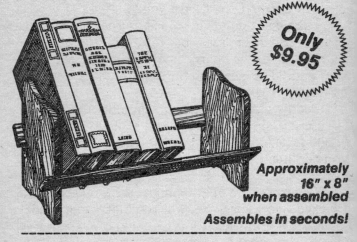

# What readers say about Harlequin romance fiction…

"I absolutely adore Harlequin romances! They are fun and relaxing to read, and each book provides a wonderful escape."
—N.E.,* Pacific Palisades, California

"Harlequin is the best in romantic reading."
—K.G.,* Philadelphia, Pennsylvania

"Harlequins have been my passport to the world. I have been many places without ever leaving my doorstep."
—P.Z.,* Belvedere, Illinois

"My praise for the warmth and adventure your books bring into my life."
—D.F.,* Hicksville, New York

"A pleasant way to relax after a busy day."
—P.W.,* Rector, Arkansas

*Names available on request.

# Six exciting series for you every month... from Harlequin

### *Harlequin Romance*·
### The series that started it all

Tender, captivating and heartwarming...
love stories that sweep you off to faraway places
and delight you with the magic of love.

### *Harlequin Presents*·
### Powerful contemporary love stories...as individual as the women who read them

The No. 1 romance series...
exciting love stories for you, the woman of today...
a rare blend of passion and dramatic realism.

### *Harlequin Superromance*®
### It's more than romance...
### it's Harlequin Superromance

A sophisticated, contemporary romance-fiction
series, providing you with a longer,
more involving read...a richer mix of complex plots,
realism and adventure.

# Harlequin
## American Romance™
### Harlequin celebrates the American woman...

...by offering you romance stories written about American women, by American women for American women. This series offers you contemporary romances uniquely North American in flavor and appeal.

◆

# *Harlequin Temptation*™
## Passionate stories for today's woman

An exciting series of sensual, mature stories of love...dilemmas, choices, resolutions... all contemporary issues dealt with in a true-to-life fashion by some of your favorite authors.

◆

# Harlequin Intrigue™
## Because romance can be quite an adventure

Harlequin Intrigue, an innovative series that blends the romance you expect... with the unexpected. Each story has an added element of intrigue that provides a new twist to the Harlequin tradition of romance excellence.

# Harlequin Books®

PROD-A-2